POETIC JUSTICE

POETIC JUSTICE

L. A. Taylor

Walker and Company
New York

First published in the United States of America in 1988 by the Walker Publishing Company, Inc.

Published simultaneously in Canada by Thomas Allen & Son Canada, Limited, Markham, Ontario.

Library of Congress Cataloging-in-Publication Data

Taylor, L. A. (Laurie Aylma), 1939–
    Poetic justice.

    I. Title.
PS3570.A943P64   1988   813'.54   87-37164
ISBN 0-8027-5701-4

Printed in the United States of America

10 9 8 7 6 5 4 3 2 1

The lines of poetry quoted in this book are from the following poems:

page 42, "The Fury of Aerial Bombardment," by Richard Eberhart
page 57, Sonnet XVIII, "Shall I Compare Thee To a Summer's Day" by William Shakespeare
pages 73 and 77, "Silent Noon," by Dante Gabriel Rossetti
page 80, "The Force That Through the Green Fuse," by
    Dylan Thomas
page 129, "Drunken Old Solipsists in a Bar," by Richard Lattimore
page 161, "Renascence," by Edna St. Vincent Millay

POETIC JUSTICE, WITH HER LIFTED SCALE,
WHERE, IN NICE BALANCE, TRUTH WITH GOLD SHE
  WEIGHS,
AND SOLID PUDDING AGAINST EMPTY PRAISE.
                              —ALEXANDER POPE

Prologue

"NOTHING SO DIFFICULT AS A BEGINNING . . .
UNLESS, PERHAPS, THE END."

—BYRON, *Don Juan*

AS THE PLOW passed down the street, heaving thick white curds of snow over the blackened layers of other storms, Owen Davis-Williams turned from the window and sat down at his desk. The brilliant blue of the sky was echoed there, a gloss on the stack of cheap white typing paper, and in the impressionable white walls of the room. For several minutes he sat with his forearms resting on the rounded top of his old IBM typewriter, staring at the bare linden twigs outside the doubled window. The room seemed shadowed with ghosts that walked and spoke in his mind.

Beside the typewriter lay an untidy pile of notes interleaved with old typed copy much written over in red ink, and just beyond that an orange cat had folded its paws into a tidy package and dozed in regal contentment. Davis-Williams scratched the cat under its chin, putting off work for a few more minutes to watch the jaw stretch up, the ears fold back, to listen for the cat's rough purr.

"Well, Alonzo, old chap," he sighed at last. "Shall we begin, again?" The cat half opened its eyes as Davis-Williams pulled his hand back and rolled the switch of the typewriter under his thumb. He fed one of the sheets under the roller, called up the vision of that dazzled, dusty, oppressive afternoon—just last summer!—set his fingers on the keys, and began to type:

FOREWORD

What you are reading, I write as a victim. In a sense, we were all victims of murder, and all crip-

1

pled in some way; every one of us who attended the writers' workshop that brought us together in June of 1982, and of which I was the leader, returned home unhappily aware that death hath more dominion over us than we care to think about. At the time I took the job, I thought of it as an easy way to earn a little extra money while my wife and I enjoyed a few weeks at a comfortable resort, an idea that has its ironies. But how else is a poet to manage? Certainly not by the sale of his books!

Even the neophytes in my class kept journals, notebooks, diaries. Where I have entered others' heads in this story, where I have written of things that occurred when I was not present, I have made use of these various sources—with the permission of their owners, of course. I have not troubled with footnotes, which seemed to me to break the flow of the narrative, with which decision I hope the scholars among you will concur. I may say that at times I was sorely tempted. There is a certain, often considerable, shock in viewing through another pair of eyes an event you yourself have intimately experienced; often I found it difficult to restrain myself from putting my own oar in. For the same reason—the flow of the story—I have written of myself in the third person. That decision had the unexpected side benefit of making it easier to be honest in sometimes embarrassing circumstances.

To those who consider any of us foolish to have thought and acted and felt as we did, pray remember that I have organized this book in the manner of a work of fiction, several months of our lives pruned and bullied into a continuous narrative light enough to hold in your hands, to read in an evening. Events as we encounter them are discontinuous, confusing, often senseless; we may not see the thread that connects one incident to another for days or even years, if ever; we may never discover, let alone bridge, the gulf between how things were and how we thought they were, yet this is the very area in which the reader expects everything made plain for him. I have done my best to make things plain, yet I must remind you that facts are not truth, they are only the armature upon which truth is sculpted. What I had to work with here was only facts, and emotional ones at that.

With that plea to you to remember our common, erring humanity, enough putting off. Let us begin.

Davis-Williams sat and read over what he had written with profound dissatisfaction. He had begun to sound positively Victorian. Oh, well. Perhaps things would improve when he got out of the wretched first person singular. . . .

Part One

1

SOME OF THE heat of the street, where the empty Sunday sidewalks had baked in mid-June sunlight since early morning, pushed through the glass doors of the bus terminal with the dark-haired woman. Behind her the doors swung shut, damping the growl of the buses shimmering in their fumes.

Like the woman, most passengers preferred the wintry blast of the air-conditioning laboring to maintain Minnesota's reputation for frigid weather to the prospect of stifling outdoors. They were, she saw, the usual mixture. Strangers headed east or west sprawled on the sticky plastic seats or paced, with tiny ripping noises at each step, from one end of the waiting room to the other. A few drifters had taken shelter from the sweltering afternoon. On the far side of the room, a pair of furry young men in cut-off jeans leaned against the wall beside the pop machine and ogled every female under thirty, while nearby a plump, frizzy blonde sporting—backward—a T-shirt emblazoned with QUESTION AUTHORITY stood with her weight on one foot and tapped the other.

The dark-haired woman carried her suitcase to the nearest row of seats and lowered herself into one, knees and ankles neatly together. Her lips disappeared as she moistened them; although she looked to be on the brink of middle age, she wore no makeup. The doors continued to swing. Gusts of hot air entered with each new passenger, one a long-faced woman whose frown changed to a smile as she spotted the frizzy blonde and crossed the room waving her free hand.

The blonde and her friend sat down near the dark-haired woman and embarked upon a fierce discussion of the poetry workshop they were about to attend. The older woman glanced briefly at them as she leaned forward to look at the clock. Just past noon. She folded her hands, pale, long-fingered hands on which the veins seemed very blue, on top of a black loose-leaf notebook in her lap. When the metallic voice of the announcer called the next departure, she half rose, the notebook clasped to her chest. It was the wrong bus, after all. She relaxed into the seat.

The motion had caught the blonde girl's attention, and she stared at the notebook and then at the woman's face. "Are you going to Davis-Williams's workshop at the Summer Arts Conference, by any chance?" she demanded.

The older woman nodded.

"What's your name?" the blonde pursued.

"Anita Soderstrom."

"Have I heard of you?"

The woman smiled, a smile that began with her eyes and barely touched her mouth. "I doubt it."

"Have you published?" the blonde's friend asked, turning round in her seat.

"Only a little." Anita shifted her grip on the notebook. "Have you?"

"Oh, yes, scads," the young woman replied, her face longer than ever, since in fact she had published exactly three poems, two of them in her church bulletin. "I'm Miriam Dubbins. You may call me Mim."

Anita nodded and raised her eyebrows at the frizzy blonde. "Sue Falk," the girl said, grudgingly, although she had started the conversation. "And no, I haven't published anything. Yet."

"Maybe you will, after this."

The blonde shrugged and looked away. Her friend, after another glance at Anita, picked up the conversation where they had left off, cataloging the acquaintances they thought might be at the workshop. A new influx of passengers from the hot street brought shouts of recognition from some of the waiting crowd. One more poet, to judge by the gush of conversation, and some potters going to the other workshop of this session of the Arts Conference. The dark-haired woman sat quietly, her fingers tracing the slight indentation that formed a border to the pebbly surface of the notebook cover. No one else spoke to her.

The loudspeaker clicked again: the announcer called the coach for Brainerd, Minnesota, and points north. As the list reached Coleridge, a good part of the crowd surged toward the doors. Outside, three buses now waited; the crowd swayed back and forth like a single questing animal until the driver of the bus farthest left took a gulp of the poisonous air and yelled that his was the bus for Brainerd. The appearance of unity dissolved into a flurry of activity. Suitcases were handed into the luggage bin under the seats, tickets checked. Passengers climbed into the bus.

Not even Sue or Mim took any notice as Anita slid into a window seat near the back and slowly leafed through her notebook. It held a thin sheaf of perfectly typed poems, all in the traditional forms demanded by Owen Davis-Williams, who was to lead the workshop, and quite a lot of blank lined paper. One of the furry young men plumped down in the seat beside her, glanced at the notebook without interest, and flipped open an old issue of *Ceramics Monthly*. In the seat ahead, two bearded youths argued heatedly about the infield fly rule, something to do with the baseball game the Minnesota Twins were losing, heard over the radio one of them waved above his head. Across the aisle, Sue and Mim slumped with their feet pressed against the back of the seats ahead of them, bored already. Sue had bought a can of Tab in the station and sipped at it once in a while. She wiped a ring of condensation from her bare left knee as the driver got into his seat and adjusted the mirrors.

Miriam checked the bus for people she knew: not as many as she'd hoped. That weird woman with the bun in her hair was a few seats back, writing in her notebook. What about? Mim wondered. Steve McCready was shouting about something in the seat ahead of her; *God, let him keep his hands to himself!* she prayed without thinking. A dim little creature she'd seen at several readings had grabbed a front seat. What was the kid's name? Dawn something. Anyone else? Her head swiveled again.

A loud clunk sounded at the front of the bus and Miriam turned to stare. A girl of about twenty mounted the steps, bumping her suitcase ahead of her.

"That'll have to go under, miss," the driver said. He slipped out of his seat. The girl smiled a slow, red-lipped smile and pushed the case toward him. He carried it back down the steps with a sigh even Mim could hear.

"Oh, shit." Sue rested the can of Tab on her knee again. "Here comes trouble."

"Who is she?"

"You don't know her? That's Roz Haddad."

Roz surveyed the other passengers, standing behind the white line set into the floor at the front of the bus as if it were a row of footlights. Her tongue moved languorously over her glossy lipstick. Her hips swayed slightly although neither her feet nor the bus moved. The luggage compartment door slammed, sending a shudder through the bus.

On that signal, Roz started down the aisle. She tossed her hair back with a little wriggle and swayed past the first four rows of seats on bright platform sandals, her narrow waist and hips rocking smoothly, the black curls bouncing on slim tanned shoulders. Every male eye missed these details, fastened instead on the perilously low neckline of her lacy blouse. The baseball argument died in mid-sentence and the radio, still emitting the laconic voice of the play-by-play man, sank into a lap. The Twins' infield executed a perfect double error and nobody even groaned.

Roz arched her brows. Her eyes, very dark and rimmed with brown liner, met those of every man who looked her in the face. She smiled at each of them. At last, with a brilliant flash of her large, white, splendidly even teeth, she slithered into a seat next to a gray-haired farmer who, having once spent eight years at the University of Minnesota acquiring a doctorate in agricultural management, was easily mistaken for a poet. By the time she had discovered her error, the wide steering wheel was already spinning back after the turn onto the freeway. The curve of her glossy red lips faltered for a moment, and then Roz half shrugged and settled back to make her flirtatious best of it.

Three seats back and across the aisle, Anita Soderstrom smiled as the flowery scent of Roz's perfume gradually overpowered the stale-cigar atmosphere of the bus. Her seatmate let out a whistling sigh, which she recorded, and opened his magazine muttering something uncomplimentary about nonfunctional potters. Anita studied him for a moment and wrote that down, too.

Well into the suburbs by then, the bus hurtled north along the tan highway toward the resort that would be the site of the Summer Arts Conference. Next to the farmer, Rozlynne Haddad concealed her disappointment, brown eyes shining and chin tilted at an angle long practiced in her bedroom mirror. She spilled a hundred questions about the fields rolling by, and let the farmer's answers flow over her as she silently daydreamed. Her plans for the coming two weeks seemed to her gratifying, if not overly pleasant, in prospect. She didn't associate them even remotely with any kind of danger.

Davis-Williams stopped typing and cracked his knuckles one by one. He assembled the pages he had finished and compared them to the notes from which he had been working. "Not too bad, Alonzo," he sighed. "Better than the first few tries, at least." The cat began to purr without opening its eyes.

"A good strong cup of coffee, and then we'll get cracking on Chapter Two, shall we?" He stood and looked out the window for a moment, his expression of satisfaction fading slowly into sadness.

2

THE BUS CONTINUED north and west, on narrower roads, now, toward Bemidji and eventually Grand Forks, North Dakota. Before reaching either of those cities it stopped at a dusty intersection indentified by a green highway sign as Coleridge, MN, pop. 192, to disgorge a dozen or so poets and potters into the sunlight that illuminated the aluminum ridges of Gracie's Diner. Seven Slopes, the resort where the conference was to be held, had promised a shuttle to meet any passengers coming into Coleridge, but when the intercity bus roared away from the curb it left only one vehicle in sight, a battered Chevy pickup truck that looked unpromising.

One of the poets produced a copy of the conference brochure to confirm that everyone had remembered rightly. "Maybe they know something in the diner," he suggested. "I'll go in and see what's up."

He pushed into the building to find the room with its grill and four small booths hotter than the outdoors, despite the wheezing air conditioner over the door. Inside it smelled of sizzled grease. At the counter, a thick-waisted woman, maybe Gracie herself, looked up from a confession magazine.

"Bus be along in a minute," she said. "I just called 'em up."

"Thanks." The poet wavered on one foot. Outside the window with its faint screen of sunlit dust, the others stood about, looking down the road.

"We got iced tea, root beer, orange pop, Pepsi. . . ."

"Thanks," the poet repeated. He opened the door a crack. "It's on the way," he said through the opening, and let the door fall shut. "What about some iced tea to go?" he asked Gracie.

"Sure." She dragged on a cigarette that had been balanced on the edge of the counter, put it back, and scooped ice into a styrofoam cup. A shadow fell across the window, and the door opened.

"What's that?" the newcomer asked.

"Iced tea," Gracie said decisively. "We got root beer, orange pop, Pepsi . . ."

Miraculously, everyone who wanted a cold drink after the long dry bus ride had time to be served, and still the shuttle to Seven Slopes had not appeared. The group shifted about the diner door, paced the length of the cracked sidewalk, or perched on suitcases. When repeated neck-stretchings and peerings down the road still failed to produce the desired transportation, they began tentatively to introduce themselves to one another.

Anita Soderstrom, pressed into the slim rectangle of shade cast by the air conditioner, squinted into the light. "I thought there'd be more students," she ventured as Sue and Mim drifted past her.

Mim turned back. "Oh, sure. Davis-Williams always draws a crowd. People come from all over, driving mostly." She stopped to wipe the sweat from her cheeks onto her T-shirt-covered shoulders. "The older people almost always drive."

"How come you didn't?" Sue asked Anita.

"I don't have a car."

Sue shrugged, as if the heat had made it too much trouble to pursue her unpleasantness, and turned away.

"God, I need a cigarette," Roz remarked. She glanced expectantly at a small knot of men near her. One of them produced a crushed pack of Camels and she took one. "I'm Roz," she said, "Who are you?"

"Steve McCready." He sounded puzzled, and Sue Falk looked over her shoulder to examine his face.

"Well, thanks for the cigarette, Steve," Roz said. She leaned forward to accept the light he struck for her, while Sue watched with narrowed eyes.

"On the make," Mim said, pleased to figure out why Sue's elbow had jabbed her in the ribs.

"Congratulations," Sue murmured. "You're fast today. What did I tell you when she got on the bus?" Mim sighed softly through her nose. Maybe two weeks with Sue hadn't been such a good idea. . . . "Notice, he's wearing a ring," Sue was saying. Mim watched the glint of gold on the left hand returning the matches to the pants pocket, jolted to realize that Sue must not know Steve. But then, what did it matter? All this sorting people out, what difference did it make? She turned to look down the road for the bus again, so she missed whatever Roz did next. When she felt Sue's elbow nudge her spine, she turned back to see Steve McCready rolling his handkerchief into a thick blue circle. He nestled it into his blond-brown curls with the sober absorption of a child adjusting his halo at a Christmas pageant, balanced his suitcase on his head, and swung away down the road toward Seven Slopes with his shirt sweat-soldered to his back. Roz trailed wistfully after him a step or two. She stopped and drew heavily on the cigarette, then glanced over the remaining men.

"What'd I tell you?" asked Sue, with great satisfaction. Mim drew away from her friend, telling herself it was because of the heat; Sue was just standing too close. She forced herself to list the contents of her suitcase, to be sure she had forgotten nothing.

The resort's shuttle proved to be a truncated school bus painted an improbable pink. The group watched in some doubt as it wheezed and clattered up the perfectly smooth road along which the intercity bus had carried them and ground to a stop. A wizened Indian with long black braids motioned them onto the bus, scratching absently at his chest between the buttons of his shirt as they filed up the three steps.

"Sit down, eh?" he yelled into the back of the bus, and the vehicle leaped forward four or five times, gaining speed. It careened left a few hundred yards from the intersection and followed a narrow blacktop drive along the rush-muffled edge of a lake, where water lilies raised their yellow torches above the broad hearts of their leaves, a fish surfaced briefly to snap at a low-flying insect, bitterns were startled into upright immobility by the clatter of the bus.

The road soon turned away from the lake and up a low hill, where the bus whizzed between aspens and clean-smelling firs. The sun had by now dropped far enough to stripe the blacktop with light, and a red squirrel scolded from a branch, a snip of its bird-like buzz coming in the open windows. Bunchberry flowers gleamed along the edge of the trees.

The bus rounded another bend. The trees fell away from the road, so that Dawn Atkins, sitting in the front seat, felt almost decanted into space as the road widened into a large lot in which a surprising number of cars was parked. To the left, the woods sprang open upon a grassy slope that extended to a rim of trees through which the lake glittered, and then the bus sprayed gravel and the doors banged open in front of the lodge. *"Nous sommes arrivès,"* shouted the driver. People at the front of the bus stood up and reached for their belongings.

A moose head mounted on a rough stone wall dominated the lobby at Seven Slopes Lodge, its benign and glassy gaze not at all startled by the sweaty cluster of new arrivals. Some kindly taxidermist had turned its head so that it could stare out at the long plunge of lawn

16

below, perhaps to dream of foraging in the shallows of the lake. On the opposite end of the narrow room over which the moose presided two clerks got busy at the registration desk.

Poets and potters managed to sort themselves into rough queues to have their rooms assigned. Someone made the ritual comment about the speed with which the moose had hit the wall. Among the groans and giggles Sue and Mim demanded to be put in the same room, although they hadn't made their reservations at the same time, as the brochure suggested—or rather, Sue demanded and Miriam failed to protest. They bore their keys away and Anita stepped up to the desk.

"You'll share with Miss Haddad, then," the clerk sighed. "At least we came out even."

"Fine." Anita signed the card and picked up her key to see Roz standing at the map of the resort posted on a nearby wall, glancing from her key tag to the map and back again.

"They're color-coded," Roz said. "I guess the yellow tag means I'm in the annex. You're sharing with me?" When Anita nodded, Roz hefted her bag and carried it down the hall toward the side door without the faintest wobble of her ankles on the high-heeled sandals. At the door she leaned the release bar down with her rump and they stepped out into the pungent scent of the blue spruces planted along the path.

"Ugh, gravel," Roz said. She stepped up onto the flat wooden curb of the path and teetered along with her suitcase held in both arms. The heat had penetrated even beneath the evergreens, and both women were too dispirited to say much. Roz followed Anita into the room and flipped on the air conditioner. "That should improve things," she remarked.

The room could have been anywhere in North America: motel standard. A single plastic-upholstered chair squatted near the wide window beside the door. Along the bland cream left-hand wall were ranged two double beds, separated by a wall-hung table on which the telephone—beige, as a gesture toward luxury—and a lamp with a chipped plaster base had been placed. Beyond the beds, a corner had been cut out of the long room to enclose bathtub and toilet, while opposite the door and exposed to the rest of the room was a sink. A clothes rod beside the sink extended from the rear wall to a little stub of wall sticking out on the right. A single long shelf on the right-hand wall, fitted with three drawers, served as dresser, desk, and stand for a gigantic television set, on which a small sign apologized for the poor reception of the two channels available in the area. "Fifty bucks a night!" Roz commented. "Want to know how to get rich?"

Anita dropped her suitcase on the farther bed and sat beside it.

"You want that bed?" Roz asked.

"I don't care."

"It's okay with me." Roz dumped her own elegant leather case onto the other bed and kicked off her high sandals with a sigh. The carpet, at least, was soft under bare feet. "When did they say dinner was?"

"There's a buffet after registration. That starts at six." Anita glanced at her watch. "A little less than an hour."

"Mind if I take a shower?"

"Sure, go ahead." Anita let herself fall backward onto the rough cotton bedspread and lay with her eyes closed, listening to Roz move about the room, closing the heavy green curtains, walking across the green shag carpet with a tired shuffle, rummaging through her suitcase.

"I won't be long," Roz said. The bathroom door closed and the water began to run. Anita opened her eyes. With the curtains closed, the light in the room was the cool green of a yard beneath high trees, or of the water lapping in the lake. She reached for her notebook and began to write. Soon the only sounds in the room were the splash of water, the whisper of the air conditioner, the faint glide of her pen, and Roz occasionally humming a snatch of melody in a mellow contralto. After a time she stopped writing and stared blankly at the curtained window.

The waterfall at the back of her mind had faded away a few minutes before, and at the click of the door latch Anita stirred and capped her pen. Roz came out of the bathroom wrapped in a towel that barely covered her from breast to behind. "All yours," she said.

Anita rightly interpreted this as a passport to the shower and slipped the notebook into her suitcase. She took out a few things and headed for the bathroom. "I'll wait for you," Roz offered.

"Thanks. I'll be quick."

Left alone, Roz dropped the towel to stand in front of her open case clad only in a pair of silky blue panties. Humming, she took out a number of garments, shaking each out and laying it carefully beside the suitcase. She came to a blue knit top and pulled it over her head, smoothing it over still-damp skin. At the mirror, she replaced her makeup.

She held first one skirt, then another, in front of her legs, and decided on the first, a blue calico that ended at her knees in a lace-edged ruffle that showed off her sleek tan. High blue sandals completed the outfit. In the bathroom, water splashed.

Roz examined the polish on her toenails and decided no one would notice that it was slightly chipped.

She rechecked her makeup, hung up her clothes, folded her underwear back into the suitcase, decorated the desk with a notebook and some pens, closed the case, and stood it under the hanging dress and skirts. She sat down in the chair beside the window, pulled the curtain aside, and peered out for a moment. She stood up. Water splashed in the bathroom.

"Jeez, she's taking long enough," Roz muttered. She tapped her fingers on the desk, hunted through her own purse and Anita's and found no cigarettes.

"Oh, hell," she sighed finally, and took Anita's notebook out of the suitcase lying so invitingly open.

The first poem stunned her.

Poetry, to Roz, was the sort of thing her father recited, standing in front of the fireplace on a winter evening, his right hand on his hip with his thumb hooked through the belt loop of his jeans, his left hand beating the rhythm like a choir director. Her father spoke of Great Writers so that no one could think of them without the capital letters, and her own submissions to the workshop . . . Roz gave her head a swift little shake, shaking her father away. This poem. This poem was about real people.

She turned the page and read the next, lips moving, left index finger tapping, the rhymes coming out as soft whispered explosions in the water-washed air.

"Just what do you think you're doing?"

Roz jumped guiltily and closed the notebook with a snap. "I—I—your poems are really great, you know?"

Anita crossed the room clutching a towel around her and snatched the notebook out of Roz's limp grasp. "That's mine. You can't read it unless I say you can."

The blaze in those gray eyes left Roz gawping. "I— well—, I—I didn't have anything to do, I—"

"You could have gone up to the lodge." Anita looked around the room. One strand of the long hair piled loosely atop her head came free and dangled onto her shoulder. Spotting the drawer under the television, she opened it and slammed the notebook into it. "If we're going to share a room," she said, "we'll have to give each other a little privacy."

"I'm sorry." *I just didn't want to go up there all by*

myself, Roz wanted to add, but the silly-kid words stuck in her throat. She wished she had a cigarette.

"I should hope so." Anita turned her back and stepped into a pair of panties, let the towel fall. "And that means leave my notebook alone, is that clear?" she continued, swinging the strand of hair out of the way as she hooked her bra.

"I said I was sorry," Roz pointed out sulkily.

Anita pulled on a slip and yanked a flowered dress over her head. "Okay," she said, her voice muffled by the fabric. She turned to face Roz as she buttoned up the front of the dress. "It goes both ways, of course. I leave your stuff alone, too."

Roz nodded. She watched as Anita ran a comb through her hair and parted it. She touched her own tight curls, gone almost kinky in the humid afternoon: Anita's hair was just the color of her own, a rich dark brown that verged on black, but perfectly straight. "How do you get your hair to stay up?" she asked, as a peace offering.

"Pins and prayer." The smile in the mirror was rueful. "I don't think I'll bother, now." Anita twisted a handful of hair at the side of her head and caught it back with a brown plastic comb, repeated the process on the other side, and lifted her hair onto her back with both hands.

Now. Roz took a deep breath. "About privacy," she said. She had sat again in the chair by the window; she gripped the arms of it so tightly that the flesh around her scarlet thumbnails went white beneath her tan. "Can we make some kind of deal, about having the room alone, once in a while?"

"Alone?"

"Yeah, you know. Like if we want to, uh, entertain?"

"A guy, you mean?"

Relieved at not having to explain, Roz nodded. It was something, anyway, that this Anita didn't have to be clued in, old as she was.

"I guess we could work something out," Anita said. She leaned against the all-purpose shelf with her arms folded. Hair down, she looked younger, less motherly, more approachable. Roz sighed.

"I collect writers," she heard herself confiding.

"Their autographs, or something?"

"No, them. In bed."

Anita stared at the younger woman. "That's bizarre," she observed. Her curiosity got the better of her. "How do you go about that?"

Roz looked down at her long fingernails. "That's why I go to these workshop things," she explained. "This is my first time out in the sticks. But I went to a real ding-a-ling convention last Easter—science fiction, lots of kids and old guys with potbellies dressed up like *Star Wars*. I got two good ones there, names you'd know."

Anita smiled, a closed smile that thinned the corners of her mouth. "I don't know much about science fiction," she said. "And how can you be so sure you can, um, collect Davis-Williams? Do you know him?"

Roz giggled. "Not yet! But he's Welsh, isn't he?" To Anita's blank face she added, "Remember Dylan Thomas. Anybody who could write a book like *Lady Chatterley's Lover* . . ."

Anita opened and closed her mouth twice, but found herself too intrigued by Roz to make the correction.

"So I go to workshops," Roz continued. "They're pretty good, at least, the ones near the cities are. I've already got—" She reeled off a list of names Anita did know. She blinked.

"Why didn't you get a single room, then?"

Roz snorted. The picture of her father rose up again, saying, *No, I'm not giving you any money to go to any damn workshop. What makes you think you could ever be a Writer? What gives you the gall to waste a Man like Owen Davis-Williams's time?* "What kind of money do you think a clerk-typist makes?" she asked. "I'll be lucky to eat, this next two weeks, let alone shell out another twenty bucks a night for a single room."

Anita's eyes wandered to Roz's leather suitcase and the row of clothes hanging above it.

"You will let me have the room, won't you?" Roz pleaded. "I mean, if I need it?"

"I don't see how I can stop you," Anita sighed. "Hang out the Do Not Disturb tag when you're, um, collecting, and give me a little warning if you can. Let's go register. We're already a little late."

"Right!" Roz bounced out of the chair. "Owen Davis-Williams, here I come!"

She rocketed through the door. Anita followed sedately, shaking her head. Something stirred in the back of her mind, a vague, half-sensual curiosity as to what the man looked like. Well, she'd find out soon enough. For Roz's sake, she hoped Owen Davis-Williams wouldn't prove grotesquely unattractive. Shame to waste all that money.

Putting the thought out of her head, she closed the door behind her and tried the knob to be sure it was locked. Ahead of her, Roz was walking balanced on the curb of the gravel path through the spruce grove, looking like a thoroughbred filly about to canter to the far end of the paddock with a toss of her head for that foolish trainer who thought he could tame her to a saddle.

3

THE MANAGEMENT OF Seven Slopes had set aside a rather pokey little room on the uphill side of the lower floor of the lodge for registering participants in the Summer Arts Conference—a nearly windowless room with the same bland cream walls as every "living unit" had. This was not, as one of the younger poets loudly maintained, a reflection of the management's opinion of the place of the arts in society, but a function of the amount of money the conference chairman had to spend. Perhaps that was also a reflection of the place of the arts in society, but not so direct a one as the poet imagined.

A long table had been set up at the far end of the room as a sign-in desk, but people were clustered so thickly around it that it couldn't be seen from the doorway. Roz plunged into the press. Anita hesitated, and discovered that she was standing next to Steve McCready, who had combed his beard and put on fresh jeans. "I didn't realize there'd be such a crowd," she remarked.

"Twenty poets and twenty-five potters is the rumor," he said. "Which are you?"

"Poet," Anita said. "At least, that's what I've signed up as."

McCready's teeth flashed in his beard. "I know what you mean—writing's a tough act, isn't it?" he said, rather surprising Anita, who had added the disclaimer just to be polite. "We were supposed to have a preliminary meeting with Davis-Williams tonight, but he's not coming until tomorrow. His wife's sick, or something."

"That'd be a headache."

Anita glanced to her right, to see Sue Falk, the backward T-shirt pulled even tighter under her plump arms and stained with sweat. "She's the kind that gets inconvenient headaches," Sue explained. "Oh, she's a winner! Wait'll you meet her. Teddibly Brritish, don't you know," said Sue, who had seen the woman exactly once, at a distance. "Looks like Prince Charles in drag."

"She's coming, then?" Steve asked.

"She's coming." Sue nodded vigorously in her own support. "She wouldn't let him out alone, not without a leash." She drifted away in the direction of the sign-in table, where the crowd had thinned.

"Shall we go and do likewise?" Steve asked Anita. He led the way toward the table, cutting a swathe for this little sister-ish woman to follow in. God, and thirty-five if she was a day. "You'll like Owen," he said over his shoulder. "He's kind of a stuffed shirt, but he's a great teacher."

"Hi," Roz said to Anita. "I thought you got lost."

"Not me," Anita demurred. "Did you know Davis-Williams is delayed?"

"So I hear." Roz didn't seem at all fazed. "Has to wait for his wife to get done with a headache."

"You might have your work cut out for you."

"Oh, I know about his wife," Roz said jauntily. "That just makes it more of a challenge."

Anita's eyebrows lifted. The next two weeks might prove interesting in a different way than she had hoped. She found herself shoved up against the sign-in table, somebody thrusting forms into her hands. The average age of her fellow students had increased dramatically over what it had seemed on the bus, she noticed with satisfaction. Most of the younger people seemed to know one another. Students together?

With a feeling of having been transported back in time,

she filled out the required three forms, pressing hard with the ball point pen, and handed them back.

"Poets meet in the Loft Bar," said the woman in charge of the forms. "Six-thirty, sharp. Grab something to eat on the way."

"Will Professor Davis-Williams be there?"

"Not tonight. He'll make it by morning, though." The woman was already looking at the next person in line as she finished the sentence. Anita shouldered her way out of the conference room and walked slowly through the lodge, looking for the buffet. She'd lost Roz somewhere.

Roast beef sandwich in hand, she found the Loft Bar up a rustic staircase opposite a sign that pointed downward to the dining room. It wasn't a loft, not really, just a single large room that straddled the width of the building and looked just as tacked-on as it was. Like most of the lobby, it was paneled in rough cedar. The function of the moose head had been taken over by the front fifth of an eight-point buck that gazed at a spot on the other side of the room and succeeded in looking as if it were about to yawn. A few people sat at small square tables near the head of the stairs, talking as if they knew one another. No one was tending bar; a sign hastily printed with a Magic Marker announced that the bar was closed until seven-thirty, but the downstairs bar was open.

Bright windows at the other end of the long room caught Anita's eye. She went over to them, shading her eyes against the glare of the sun, to find that the bar overlooked the long sweep of cropped grass. From this height the lake beyond the fringe of trees was spangled with sun. A canoe cut slowly across the brilliant water, leaving a dark line that diffused like ink into wet paper. To the right, the annex, with its cedar siding and bright yellow doors, peeked through the tops of the spruces. Someone was cutting across the lawn instead of following the gravel path; he reached the terrace and went out of sight below the first-floor roofline. A door squealed.

The brochure had promised swimming, giving the definite impression of sand trucked in to make a beach of the mucky lakeshore. Instead, an unnaturally blue pool nestled in the angle between the left-hand, southern wing and the parking lot. Anita tucked one leg beneath her and sat sideways on the cushioned window seat to wait, idly watching a couple of teenagers horse around on the mini-golf course down the slope from the pool as she finished her sandwich.

The voices of Sue and Mim and Steve McCready sounded in the stairwell, and a moment later their heads emerged behind the railing. Anita nodded, but they were too engrossed in what they were saying to notice. She turned back to the window. The teenagers were now standing, hands on hips, tossing their heads vehemently at each other. Roz came up the stairs and joined the other three, and at the sound of her low voice Anita turned.

"Bug off, Haddad," Sue said, not bothering to shift from her sprawl in one of the little chairs.

"Well!" Roz arched her brows and lifted one shoulder. "You're certainly friendly."

"Don't you forget it."

Roz smiled. "Don't worry, sweet Sue," she said. *"I'm* not gonna try to cut you out with Miriam."

Mim, perched tidily opposite Sue, flushed. "Can it, Roz," Steve McCready said. He shifted his chair so that his shoulder was toward Roz, who tilted her head and stared at him for a moment, then spun on one of her blue wedge heels and sauntered over to another of the bearded young men. This one seemed more receptive.

"I could just kill her, couldn't you?" Mim said loudly.

The same young woman who had taken the registration forms thumped up the stairs two at a time, somewhat red in the face. The clock over the bar read ten to seven. She climbed onto a chair, calling for attention, but had little to say: told them what they should have brought with them—the letter from Davis-Williams had already told them that—announced that Professor Davis-Williams regretted that he would not arrive until late that night, told them that the buffet was still open for anyone who might have missed it, and hopped off the chair in time to avoid the stampede of still-starving poets.

Several hours later, the sunlight had faded to a deep purple in the western windows: the Loft Bar looked entirely different. The cedar paneling languished in the cool blue light of the bar, and the stag's eyes glinted blue under the spreading shadows of his antlers. Roz Haddad clasped her hands around half a glass of beer and gazed past the jammed dance floor at the silhouettes of the spruces against the dim sky. A waiter edged past, tray held high.

"More beer?" Roz asked Anita.

"No, thanks. I want to go soon."

"Oh, please, stick with me," Roz begged. "I need the company."

"I thought you were looking for action," Anita said, her voice almost drowned by the thump of the band.

"Not yet." Roz leaned over to shout into Anita's ear. "I don't want to louse things up with . . . *you* know."

Anita half grinned. The driving rhythm, almost forgotten in the past few years, twitched in her ankles, and even the cigarette smoke didn't seem as objectionable as usual. So, why not? "Okay," she said. "I'll stay."

The band began blaring a medley of old Elvis Presley songs and one of the other poets, a man in his forties, stopped at the table and gestured at the dance floor. Roz glanced at his wife, sitting three tables away, and got up.

"This one's safe," she said into Anita's ear, as if she felt she needed an excuse.

Partly for Roz, partly to explore a new, mild, odd sense of adventure beginning, Anita stuck it out, turning down several invitations to dance before she was left alone to watch the others. A bronzed couple in elegant clothing more suited to, say, St. Tropez than to northern Minnesota caught her eye. Near them a boy trying to grow a beard and failing except for half a dozen curly sprouts provided a delicious contrast: bandannas tied around his head and one thigh, a clumsy hop of a dancing style. A fine-boned girl with eyes as distant as the stag's whirled past. At the next table, a little boy slept as if abandoned, with his head on the sticky wood and his mouth open.

Somehow it had become quarter to one and the band began to fold up. "Now to get away from these guys," Roz said. "You coming?" She stood up and picked at her skirt to free it from her sweat-damp legs.

"And how." Anita shouldered her purse strap. "We can cut across the lawn," she said.

"Hey, you're not going!" shouted a fat man with a tiny pink mouth. Roz flashed him her glossiest smile and nodded. Odd, Anita thought. She was almost certain she'd seen the man leave earlier, with the St. Tropez couple. Trip to the john, maybe. She shook off a groping hand as she and Roz made their way among the tables to the stairs. Half an hour to closing, and not many women left. These guys were going to have to work hard for whatever they got.

"Jeez," Roz said, as they reached the bottom of the stairs. "What did they do, bring a field trip from Stillwater Prison? I think I've got a couple of hands still stuck to me."

"Possibly."

"How do we get to the lawn?"

"Through the dining room and across the terrace."

They went down one more flight and through the dimmed dining room. A pair of waitresses chatting at the cash register nodded as Roz and Anita pushed through the big double doors into the cool night. The soft yellow light of the dining room, where moths bent on suicide zoomed back and forth, faded into darkness halfway across the terrace. Roz's high sandals clacked on the flagstones. A moment later they left the paving behind, and the swish of their feet through the short grass was almost drowned by insect song. Anita was listening idly to one particular cricket and wondering how close they'd come before it shut up, when Roz yelped and clutched her arm.

"Anita," she whispered. "Look at the sky! What's happening? What's wrong with it?"

Anita looked up but saw nothing wrong: just the thick summer sky drooping under its burden of stars. "What do you mean?" she asked.

"All that light! What is it? Look, there's a whole band of it! Is it smoke?"

"Roz." Anita scratched one ankle with the edge of her other sandal. "That's the Milky Way. Haven't you ever seen the stars before, for heaven's sake?"

The younger woman stood still, her upraised face pale. "I guess not," she breathed. She didn't move, although a whining chorus announced that the mosquitoes had found them. After some time, Anita tugged at her arm and led her to the annex as if guiding a blind girl. "Watch the step," she said, opening the door and flipping on the light.

Roz stumbled blinking into the room and flopped down on the near bed. "All this time, I thought the Milky Way was just a candy bar," she marveled.

*   *   *

Half an hour later, their lights went out. Half an hour after that, almost all of the lights in the lodge had also darkened, leaving only the few outside lamps that relieved the darkness of the entrance and the path from lodge to annex. Human sounds subsided. The night was left to the insects and to one loon whose cry echoed over the lake.

The man who had danced with Roz made love to his wife, who knew perfectly well where he had found his new energy, and enjoyed it anyway.

A bearded man in his mid-thirties, there to find a way to free his heart to write his anguish into poetry, woke sweating and shaking from an old nightmare of red fire and a rain of human flesh. "God," he groaned into his pillow. "Don't let me flashback here."

Sue and Miriam lay in the dark, Sue whispering the best of the gossip she'd collected that evening until Mim began to snore lightly from the other bed. When she was sure that Mim was asleep, Sue reached for the telephone, dialed, and whispered into it. A few seconds later she put it down and lay back with a smile.

An owl stooped upon a careless rabbit in the darkened parking lot and soared away, leaving only a smear of blood and a few round, greenish pellets to mark the spot. The lights of Davis-Williams's car caught the bird as it rose, but he was too weary even to exclaim. He parked the car and he and Doris carried their bags into the lodge. The desk clerk, after signing them in and handing over their keys, put his head down on the desk for just a second, and raised it blearily half an hour later.

As the night wore on, quiet shadows moved through the starlit dark, each intent upon its own business, and only two of them belonged to the bears raiding the garbage dump.

4

GIVEN THAT IT was Doris's headache that had delayed their departure from Minneapolis until the last possible moment, requiring Davis-Williams to drive late into the night in order to arrive at the workshop in time, it seemed grossly unfair that she should recover so quickly as to be first down to breakfast—and that despite the time she took over her hair. In fact, she was just finishing her last triangle of toast as Davis-Williams joined her.

"Are any of these yours, Owen?" she asked, sweeping the hand with the scrap of toast to include everyone in the dining room.

Davis-Williams looked about. The two blond beards in the far corner looked somewhat familiar, but then, all those blond beards looked alike, whether in winter plumage of plaid flannel or summer plumage of T-shirts adorned with cheeky mottoes. He saw, with a pang as their faces brought home to him what their names had not, Suzanne Falk talking to Miriam Dubbins on the terrace, where a few umbrellaed tables had been set out. What, dear Muse, have I done to deserve those two *again?* he wondered. With them was a girl wearing a white elasticized fabric band not quite broad enough to cover her breasts, very short short-shorts, wedge-heeled sandals in a sinful shade of scarlet, and most probably nothing else. Black, tousled hair, very red lips and what looked like a couple of blacked eyes but was more probably makeup. A long, lean expanse of sleek tanned belly: he felt keenly the absence of a jewel in her navel. If that one's mine, he decided, I shall call her The Body. His eyes roved over the other guests. A family of yellow-haired hiking types, surely not his, several studenty-looking specimens, and sundry others with nothing much to make one take notice. He felt a vague sense of loss that he could find no interest moving within him. Then a man sitting alone caught his eye, a man with a small, cruel, pink mouth trapped between soft folds of flesh that ran from the corners of his nose to his jawline, wearing a knit shirt that looked starched. He shuddered. Not mine, he fervently hoped.

"Those two fattish ones on the terrace are mine, alas," he told his wife. "The rest, I don't know."

Doris regarded the trio on the terrace with her give-away-nothing mask. Fattish they might be, but they had upon them the glow of youth: no wrinkles, no gray hairs to be plucked out with a tiny pain as penance for rejecting oneself, breasts that stood high without architectural assistance so far as she could tell, and doubtless they had no concern about wetting themselves when they laughed heartily, as two of them were doing now. And the third was fattish only in the most alluring places. "And that one with them?" she asked, her tone casual. She inspected the bottom of her cup and found it empty, poured two or three drops out of the little silver teapot, and looked about for the waitress. "She looks the sort not to trust, quite, don't you think?"

The question was lost on her husband. "What do you mean?" he murmured, distracted by the shining photograph of bacon and eggs in the menu, a picture he knew from experience could only have been taken almost anywhere but at Seven Slopes, although the photographer had taken care to match the crockery and to place it upon a deep blue cloth like the one gritty with crumbs under his left hand.

"One doesn't know what might rub off if one got too close, does one?" Doris continued.

"Mmmm," said her husband.

"I hope I shan't have to find out," Doris went on, with an artistic shiver. "Even indirectly."

"I don't see why you should," Davis-Williams replied, fixing his wife with a stare intended to stop this game.

"Nonetheless, I think I'll keep you company while you eat." Doris succeeded in signaling the waitress and ordered more toast and a second pot of tea. "And please, put the bag in the pot in the kitchen," she instructed. "And the water wants to be right on the boil, not just hot." The waitress nodded exactly as if she intended to bring the tea already steeping and looked at Davis-Williams, who succumbed to the fraudulent photograph and ordered bacon and eggs, sunnyside up.

He ignored Doris watching him from the other side of the table and put his mind instead to the poems that had been forwarded to him by the Summer Arts Conference chairman. Yes. Sue and Miriam . . . what was that ridiculous name she liked to be called by? Mim. Sue and Mim had had their wretched efforts in the first batch, he recalled. He hadn't nerved himself for a second look at them yet. Have to rectify that by ten o'clock, although he could probably provide a reasonable critique without ever reading the things.

Twenty students in this round. So far, all but one of them nothing to write home about. But that one . . . that one . . . ah! Almost enough to make it worth these summer workshops, something for the mind as well as for the wallet. He smiled, unaware of Doris's sharp glance.

"What's amusing, Owen?"

He brought himself back to the table to discover that his breakfast had been served, and he had even eaten half a piece of toast and some of the abominable egg. He blinked at Doris and let his gaze drift upward. The Body, out on the terrace, was certainly staring at him. Did she . . . no. Not so many years ago, he'd have thought she found him irresistably attractive, but now, he told himself sternly, it's getting time to face the fact of age: she was another of his students.

Suzanne and Miriam turned. Horrors, were all three of those girls about to waylay him at his breakfast? He hastily looked at his plate, where the bacon lay half burnt and half pale and flabby and the remaining egg minded its own business quite unaware of having been cooked to a thick yellow frazzle.

The three on the terrace rose and began to move separately but purposefully toward the doors to the dining room.

"Let's go up," Davis-Williams said. "I've done with this."

"I still have my tea," Doris objected.

"Bring it along." He stood up and headed for the cash register, heedless of the paper napkin that glided under the table. The waitress angled to intercept him, waving his check. He added a suitable figure for her tip and signed the check with his room number. She grinned. Well she might: he could afford to be generous with the conference's money. Were those girls still after him?

A swift reconnaissance over his shoulder proved they were. Davis-Williams scooted for the stairs and took them two at a time despite his fifty years, arrived panting at his room, thrust the key into the lock and whipped through the door, closed it and leaned against it. Until ten o'clock, his time was technically his own, and he meant to keep it so: nothing on earth could induce him to put up with Suzanne or Miriam so much as one second sooner.

"Owen, let me in," Doris said plaintively, through the

door. He opened it wide enough for her to slide through it sideways and shut and locked it behind her.

"Shh!" He took the cup and teapot from her and set them on the bedside table.

"What's got into you? Have you seen a ghost?"

"Worse. Dubbins and Falk."

"It sounds like a comedy turn," Doris observed.

"Only for one with a different sense of humor to mine," Davis-Williams said. "They are without doubt the worst manglers of English prosody I have ever encountered. It's quite enough simply to think of them committing verse within this landscape, and just now they showed every sign of coming up to me to say hello."

"You *are* unfriendly." Doris poured the tea into her cup, where it steamed feebly. Anemic. Perhaps this northern water couldn't be made to boil properly.

"That other one was coming, too."

"The one bursting out of her clothes?" Doris glanced at her watch. "Well, your time's your own until ten, and you can't be expected to hold yourself ready to entertain anyone who comes along, then, can you?" She peered into the mirror over the dressing table and patted her graying blonde hair, which was perfectly in place, as might be expected considering how long she had spent twisting it into a chignon and plaiting a bit to wrap round the bun and hide the hairpins.

Davis-Williams consulted his own watch. "I've got forty-five minutes. I think I'll read over that stuff that came in the mail yesterday, so I'll know what I'm up against."

Doris made a face into the glass and announced that she was going to sit on the terrace. He put up the chain behind her and, sighing, got the new poems out of their envelope and sank into the one comfortable chair in the room.

I wandered over hill and dale, he read. *Just like a*

lonely little cloud. His eyes flicked to the top of the sheet. Rozlynne Haddad. Dear God, did she think he hadn't read Wordsworth? *And all at once I laughed out loud,* she had continued, *at all the flowers in the vale.* Well, she had preserved the rhyme, at least, and it did scan properly. And she'd found the early nineteenth century, of which he supposed he should be glad. What is the state of civilization, he wondered sadly, when such minor considerations can take the edge off plagiarism? He scrawled *Don't copy!!* in red ink across the face of the page, skipped over the rest of her offerings—a little Browning, something by the shores of Gitchee Goomee fellow—and decided to console himself with Anita Soderstrom's three sonnets.

Now, there was grace! Wordsworth himself . . . would have done them better, to be honest. But even Wordsworth would have had nothing to shame him in these . . . Davis-Williams shook himself and shuffled through the remaining pages one more time. As he had suspected, he needn't have troubled to read either Dubbins or Falk; neither had a bit more wit than they'd had last winter. Lord, he was tired after that drive, and this was only the first of three two-week sessions, tiring in themselves. . . .

The lounge where the poetry workshop was scheduled to meet this first morning was still empty when Davis-Williams descended the four steps into it, twenty minutes later. Pity they had to meet first in this cheerless little room ringed with dull black vinyl sofas, with all the glinting light out-of-doors, the grass glittering in the breeze that swept off the lake. Sighing, he took a seat on the raised hearth of the cold fireplace to wait for the students to straggle in and carefully arranged his long legs with one casual ankle across the other knee to conceal the opening-class jitters that brought a fine tremor to his cool, perspiring hands and shortened and shallowed his breathing, even after all these years.

He had an excellent idea of what he looked like. A tall, lanky man, Davis-Williams cultivated a reddish tuft of beard that, together with a classic nose, good cheekbones and a rounded forehead over slightly deep-set eyes, gave him some resemblance to Ezra Pound, a resemblance his colleagues sometimes remarked upon and which brought him both a spurious sort of pride—Pound was, after all, one of the century's most influential poets, and a resoundingly well-read man—and a certain embarrassment. To be honest, he could bear neither the man's fascist politics nor his poetry. Davis-Williams himself wrote in, loved, venerated, the traditional verse forms poets like Pound had almost destroyed. He wrote well enough to have been awarded a Guggenheim Fellowship for the coming year, with which he purposed to publish a fifth book of verse, a sonnet sequence he'd been working on for several years. And he had attracted a modest following of poets also working in the old forms, which afforded him great satisfaction.

He looked up as one of the bearded young men descended the steps and glanced uncertainly at him. Davis-Williams stretched his mouth into a polite smile and the youth lowered himself onto the edge of a sofa. Whoever the fellow was, he wasn't Anita Soderstrom. Who, exactly, Anita Soderstrom was, other than the author of those three exquisite sonnets, Davis-Williams didn't know.

He hoped, intensely, she would not prove to be The Body.

The other blond beard of the dining room arrived and sat on the opposite side of the room from the first. Good, good. Always nice to have a little symmetry. Now, Falk one side and Dubbins the other—they arrived as he thought of them and sat predictably side by side just opposite him, to the right of the steps—and the rest of them, sixteen to go, if they all showed up. He exchanged the minimum of pleasantries with Falk and Dubbins and took a wad of papers out of his briefcase to shut them up.

All the students did arrive by ten, while he made a show of looking through their poems: necessary, if only to keep his eyelids from drooping. The Body arrived last, more or less as he had expected, and slithered . . . well, to be accurate, she didn't slither, but she gave that sinuous impression . . . up to the fireplace, to sit on the raised hearth beside him, where she blinked her enormous brown eyes and ran the tip of a pink tongue over her red mouth. And on my right hand, he thought, annoyed. He counted heads, got twenty, and rose to introduce himself.

He knew how to use his voice, a pleasant baritone, and he used it now to soothe and encourage his students. His British accent had got a bit weathered round the edges by over twenty years of teaching in the American Midwest, but it still had its power to impress, a power that amused him and of which he took quite conscious advantage. After a few words about the workshop and about himself, words that came easily of long practice, he asked the students to introduce themselves, listening for that one name.

Not the grandmotherly woman, as he had half decided as he watched them come in and settle themselves. Another, a woman only a little older than the college crowd, thirty-three or -four at a guess. Luminous shyness, that was his first impression. If the earliest-blooming snowdrop of spring should suddenly breathe and speak, that would be Anita Soderstrom. Not that she looked at all fragile: of medium height, she was on the slender side but not of that painful skinniness some American women liked to affect. Her mass of brown hair was held back from a strong-boned, strikingly pale face by two tortoiseshell combs. Perhaps because of the heat, she had pulled the long ends into a careless ponytail held by a wide barrette. Her gray eyes seemed to look not at, but into him. She fit her writing: Davis-Williams smiled his pleasure. So taken was he by her appearance that he didn't quite catch her occupation. Something to do with computers, of all things.

He detached his thoughts reluctantly to hear what the next person had to say: a teacher. The group was well-salted with teachers looking for the two postgraduate credits that would bolster their salaries. Heavily weighted at each end of the age spectrum: the twenty-five-year-olds desperate to hold on to their jobs long enough to work up to tenure—well he knew about that!—and the fifty-five-year-olds up against the realization that their pensions were not going to stretch as far as they had thought they might. Well he knew about that, for that matter. There were three, none of them teachers, in the middle age group: Anita, a flaccid man with a lisp, and a hairy, haunted-looking brute who defiantly announced himself as a veteran of the Vietnam War and looked disappointed when no one recoiled. Much the same assortment as usual.

"For our first exercise, which will be in prose, as will many of our early exercises," he said, still standing, "let's just write a description of the person to our left. I won't be taking part in this," he added, with a hasty glance at The Body, who was purring with some sort of glee, "so you, Miss Um, will write about Mr., Mrs., Uh."

"Call me Roz," The Body said cozily.

"Yes, well. Ten minutes, everyone."

He spent the ten minutes thinking of how he would describe Anita Soderstrom, bent over her notebook and writing slowly with a bright blue felt tip pen. Those gray eyes. Not silver, exactly, what was the metal he had in

40

mind? Pewter, that was it, altogether a warmer color. That pallor . . . he hoped she wasn't ill! Perhaps she never went out in the sun? A night-shift worker, perhaps? And what to say of that heavy brown hair, save that it was heavy?

The blond beard to Anita's right praised her "deerlike grace."

"Rather a cliché, don't you think?" Davis-Williams asked gently. "Try and dig a little deeper. What else is graceful?"

A little silence. "Trees?" the beard ventured doubtfully.

"Oh, dear, no. Joyce Kilmer has ruined them forever," Davis-Williams exclaimed. "What else? Class?"

Deerlike. Cliché, yes, but an apt cliché. He had the impression that she could fade, fawnlike, into her background and from her place miss nothing. At the moment she was pink with attention, but amid the rest of the florid specimens—The Body, for instance, who had turned out to be the Wordsworth thief and was now gradually driving him off the end of the hearth by repeatedly snuggling near—Anita Soderstrom stood out by not standing out, with the exception of her poems. Watching her, as his voice automatically conducted the first of the day's sessions and the clock wound all too slowly toward noon, Davis-Williams found a strange peace welling up in him. So strong was the impression that by the time he was ready to dismiss the class and head for his room, he had already decided upon the code name she would bear in his journal. Henceforth, Anita would be Irene. Peace. Let prying Doris try to figure that one out.

While he had been talking, The Body had moved closer; he stood to escape the warm press of her thigh against his and was startled to hear her shift into the space he had just occupied. What now? Sit, and he'd land in her lap! To conceal his shock he strolled round the circle, winding up the class discussion.

A minute or so later he found he had fetched up beneath the vent for the air-conditioning, its well-remembered warning of breakdown (a warmish mist) soft upon his neck. "I see it's past the hour," he said, finishing. "Shall we meet on the terrace this afternoon, instead of here?" He collected several nods of relief. "Yes? At two-thirty, then, on the terrace."

He had started to replace his papers in his briefcase and gather up the extras of the handouts he had distributed that morning, when the conference coordinator spoke from the doorway. "I'm awfully sorry, Professor," she said, twisting her hands together in front of her Arts Conference T-shirt. "There's a problem. The police want to ask all your students about last night."

His eyes shifted to the large man in uniform standing behind the coordinator. "Problem?"

"Something . . . someone . . . something's missing. This is Deputy Bluetongue. He can explain."

Bluetongue advanced into the room and stood regarding the poets with black almond-shaped eyes somewhat sunken behind the bronzy tan of his cheekbones. "I want you to leave the room one at a time," he instructed. "My partner will ask each of you some questions, and I'll stay here to make sure you don't talk to each other."

"Oh!" Davis-Williams looked round the circle of students and sagged onto one of the vinyl sofas. "Yes, surely."

Deputy Bluetongue crossed the circle and stood before the empty fireplace, just as the poet had earlier, and said nothing more. *He looks on shock-pried faces,* Davis-Williams thought, and then remembered that Eberhart had said that of God.

Observing Bluetongue, so large, so fit, the energy

barely contained in his brown uniform, Davis-Williams could almost believe he'd used the line appropriately. He felt that he didn't dare even to ask The Body to leave his side.

5

DAVIS-WILLIAMS HAD little to offer Deputy Bluetongue's colleague, whose less remarkable name he didn't catch. Like a dutiful schoolboy, he recited what he did know: he had arrived near two-thirty that morning with his wife, had seen no unusual—indeed, not any—activity in the parking lot, and had not passed a car on the entrance road. The questioning was over in three minutes, counting his assuring the other deputy that his suspicion was correct, Davis-Williams was British. He felt singularly useless as he hurried to his room to drop his papers off. Doris wasn't there; she must already have gone to lunch.

At the door to the dining room, he scanned the crowded tables. Every guest in the lodge must be lunching here today, he thought: crime fascinates the felon in the honest man far more than it does the honestly criminal. At the windows Rozlynne Haddad waved to him and pointed at the empty seat at her table for two. He smiled or grimaced and shook his head, still searching for Doris. He was on the point of joining Martin Jonas, the ceramics professor, when he spotted his wife sitting with a younger couple, strangers, and two children. He made his way toward her, chin lifted.

"Owen, this is Judith Ammans," Doris said. "And her husband, Roger, their son, also Roger, and this is Elizabeth, their daughter. My husband, Owen."

"How d'you do?" he murmured. He drew the chair up behind his knees and sat down. It was the hiking-type couple and their children whom he'd noticed at breakfast, he realized. How had Doris become so friendly so quickly?

"They've the room next to us," Doris said. "For two weeks. Isn't that marvelous?" So. That was how she had met them. And in a moment or two it became obvious that friendliness was "their bag," along with hiking, birding (whatever that might be; he had a sudden vision of skinny Roger Ammans hunched on a branch against the moonlight with John Austin, attempting to imitate an owl. Would he flap his wings, or give a tolerable hoot?), and the careful identification of everything from roadside weeds to spiders with the aid of one or another of the grubby little books Judith produced from the backpack leaning against the legs of her chair. Yes, that would endear her to Doris, straight off. Davis-Williams stared covertly at the woman. Something about her shoulder-long hair had changed since the morning. Had she got it done, perhaps?

She noticed his furtive examination, grinned, and lifted the elastic edge of a wig. Abashed, he looked at his silverware. "Oh, don't worry," she laughed. "I use it to cover up when I've just washed the real stuff and don't want to look like a drowned rat."

"Excellent notion," Doris pronounced. "Have they questioned you, Owen?"

"Yes. Not that I could tell them anything of import. What's it all about?"

"A burglary," Judith Ammans said, her eyes sparkling. "Seventeen hundred dollars in cash, wasn't it, Roger? And some valuable jewelry, too."

"Why anyone would want to bring jewelry here, I don't know," Doris commented. "It's not that formal a place."

"You've got a couple of thousand dollars on your left ring finger right at this moment," Davis-Williams pointed out. He remembered how frightened he had felt, going into the shop to see what he could buy for seventy-five pounds, all he had been able to scrape together to buy a ring for Doris. How his heart had pumped! The clerk had hardly been obsequious, but he hadn't been exactly rude, and after half an hour of changing his mind from this to that to the other, he had walked out of the shop with the ring in a small blue box, shocked that anyone could spend an amount of money so much greater in volume than the item he had bought.

Doris gave her ring a startled glance. She used not to be able to tear her eyes from it, Davis-Williams thought. "Yes, I suppose I do," she said. "But you don't think anyone would take a wedding ring?"

"Sure," said Roger Ammans. "If it's worth a lot of money."

Doris murmured something about respect. Judith laughed. "Burglars can't be sentimental," Roger said. "I heard of a case where they cut the finger off an old lady just to get her rings."

"Can I have some more root beer?" Elizabeth asked.

"In a minute."

"I want it now."

"Honey, we have to wait for the waitress to come."

Davis-Williams, about to protest such stories in front of children, held his tongue. While Judith dealt with her pouting child, he reviewed the menu, just as if he hadn't memorized it in other years, and decided to choose the relative safety of the seafood salad. The waitress was a long time coming, the child querulous, the afternoon class approaching more rapidly than he liked. He twisted his head, trying to relax his neck muscles, and listened very little to the rumors about the burglary or to Doris's account of her morning's tramp with the family Ammans.

By the time he reached his room to pick up the class materials for the afternoon, he had to steel himself against falling onto the bed for a good sleep. Doris had put one of her pitchers of wildflowers on the dressing table, he saw when he nearly knocked it over. Almost subconsciously, he deduced that she must have walked into town to the post office or the general store, because the improvised vase blazed with the Indian paintbrush and daisies that grew along the roadside, and not the bouncing Bet and columbine of the woodland paths. What to do this afternoon, needing a rest already? He paused to think, midway in changing to a cooler pair of shorts. The meditation exercise, perhaps, or describing an object?

Brushing his hand across his face and wiping the sweat onto his clean shorts, he locked the room behind him and made for the stairs.

Out on the terrace the high squeals of the teenagers in the swimming pool darted around the wing of the lodge with the exclamatory splash of someone diving. Oblivious to the noise, Sue Falk sprawled in a chair with her head tilted back to let the sun even the tan on her neck.

"I don't know how you can stand the sun," Mim Dubbins said from the shade of an umbrella. "It's so damned hot."

Sue stopped fanning herself with her spiral-bound notebook and opened her eyes a fraction. "It's my neck," she pointed out.

Her neck, with white rings visible between the rounds of fat when she stretched it back, Mim thought. Sue ought not to go out in the sun at all. "You're just trying to look like Roz," she teased, reckless with heat. "So you can go to work on Jack Saarinen."

Sue sat up abruptly and glared at Mim, who shrank back. Too late, she remembered there were things one didn't say to Sue. "He's married," Sue said.

"Everybody's married," Mim replied, distracted into another line of thought. "But that doesn't stop Roz."

"I hope you don't think I'm another Roz! All that effing! It's too effing much!"

Oh, dear, Mim thought. I've done it again. "Besides, you'd have to stuff a couple of volley balls up your shirt," she said, to underline that it had been a joke.

No such luck. "I've got better things to do with balls than stuff them up my shirt," Sue said indignantly. Mim, whose crooked teeth had taught her how to keep a straight face, backed into silence. Sue squinted pointedly at the terrace doors, one of which flashed in the sunlight. "Here comes somebody, finally. Oh, it's Steve." She flopped one hand at him and he headed for the table she and Mim had chosen.

"He's probably going to want to move onto the grass," Steve said as he approached. "He always does."

"Bees," Mim said.

Steve looked out over the long lawn, where white heads of clover stood in the breezeless sunlight, bobbing as the bees landed on them. Little currents of warm air spurted past the thick soles of his sandals and curled over his toes. Bees or burn, he thought resignedly. And the women always preferred to burn. "Well, maybe we can get him to stay on the paving," he said. "But he likes circles, you know that."

"I hope this afternoon is better," Mim said. "He sure didn't have his usual spark this morning."

"Tired, I guess, after driving all night," Steve said. "He doesn't often drone on like that. I wonder if he saw anything with that burglary?"

"He'd have said if he did," Mim pointed out.

"Did the cops ask you a million questions, Steve?" Sue asked.

"Only about three. You know, they questioned the potters first, right in the middle of class?" he added, showing his first sign of animation. "Can you imagine? There's my wife with her thumbs in the clay, opening up a cylinder, and this guy comes up behind her and says, pardon me, may I ask you a few questions, you know that big voice, and she damn near fell off the seat. Kick wheel, too.''

"I wouldn't know," Sue said.

"I didn't realize your wife was here," Mim said. "How come you rode up on the bus?"

"She came ahead to visit her sister in Bemidji for a couple of days." Steve yawned. "Where is everybody?"

"Maybe we should go check the lounge?"

"No, it's all right," Steve said as the grandmotherly woman poked her head through the door. "Here comes Dorothy."

Most of the rest of the students arrived in the next four or five minutes, and the conversation began to buzz as if echoing the bees on the lawn. At about twenty to three, Davis-Williams backed through the terrace doors with his arms filled with stacks of stapled paper and the buzz died down.

"I've just picked up a few things I had copied for you," he explained, puffing. "So, as it looks as if everyone's here, I'll hand them out."

"Roz isn't here yet," somebody said.

Davis-Williams raised his head and looked over the group with a faintly befuddled expression. "Oh, yes. Miss Uh. Haddad, is it? Well, while we wait, perhaps we could move onto the grass, where it's cooler."

"Bees," Mim said.

"Oh, yes?" Davis-Williams stared blankly at the lawn for a moment. "Well, we'll just move into the shade, then, there near the building. We'll make a circle, shall we? Bring chairs." He grabbed the nearest empty chair by the back and dragged it behind him toward the wide shade of the building, two white scars on the flagging marking his path. He twirled the chair against the wall and dropped his stack of papers onto the pavement beside him as he sat down.

"Now, then. Miss Haddad still not here?" Davis-Williams glanced at his watch. "It's well past the hour, so we'll just begin without her. Lots of work this afternoon, class. First, I want us to spend about fifteen minutes just writing anything that comes into our heads, *but*"—he glared at them all for emphasis—"we will focus our efforts upon one object. One. Choose an object you can see—a stone, a flower, perhaps even a chair, but *not* a person, and describe it thoroughly in the most extravagant terms you can devise. Prose again, class. Now."

To set a good example, he began scribbling in his own notebook, having chosen a rainspout at the near corner of the building as his subject. Odd that he'd said that about not a person, he thought, as his pen raced along with a semiautomatic blather about summer thunderstorms. Usually he placed no strictures upon this exercise. He shifted uncomfortably on the metal chair, made a note of the skeletonized maple leaf litter that had been washed out of the downspout some days before, and thought how to describe the way the power mower had scattered it.

Miriam Dubbins watched him glance from notebook to rainspout and wondered what he could find so interesting over there. She looked unhappily at her own description of flagstones. Flat and gray. What else? Davis-Williams she could have described, in words borrowed from various sources: from Emily Dickinson, his eyes, the color of sherry left in the glass, from any of a dozen romantic novels, his hair glinting copper in the sun. Blue shadows under his eyes. Tired. That's why the juice has gone out of him, she thought. Steve's right.

Flat, gray flagstones. *Rough-surfaced,* she wrote. She remembered some slate she'd seen once, the surface rippled like water frozen by a high-speed photograph, and wondered if comparison were legal. The pock-pock of hurrying steps made her look up. Roz Haddad stumped toward the group, her mouth set in an angry pout.

"I'm sorry," she said, dragging a chair into the circle and flouncing into it with, for no apparent reason, a glare for Anita. "That jerk cop wanted to see me again."

"I'll bet he did," Sue muttered. Something going on here, Davis-Williams recognized with despair. How he hated complications! He explained the exercise to The Body and told them all to take ten minutes more at it. Please, he half prayed, let this be a nice, uncomplicated summer!

By the end of ten minutes, as he might have expected given the wet-flannel air that enveloped them, everyone had stopped writing. "Time," he said. "Who'd like to read what he's written?"

He listened to several little essays infected with heat and the general malaise, and then suggested that they read some of the poems they had brought with them. He waited, watching them scramble through their papers, and let Miriam Dubbins take first turn. She read solemnly, with the annoying trick of turning every line into a question and coming down hard on the rhyme; he concentrated with such difficulty that he was reminded of sixth-form maths, three-quarters of his life ago and four thousand miles away. Feeling slightly guilty, he called upon the class for comments.

No one found much to say. Davis-Williams scanned the circle of faces, wondering which of them had thought the poem entirely satisfactory, which had no thoughts in their heads anyway, and which simply did not know where to begin to offer suggestions for improvement. He thought perhaps Anita Soderstrom fell into this latter category. It was that sort of poem. So was Suzanne

Falk's, and during her reading he clearly saw Anita wince twice, though she hid it passably.

"Miss Soderstrom?" he asked, when he thought the silence after Sue's poem had gone on long enough. "What about one of yours?"

"Oh!" Anita's mouth fell open, as if she had not expected any interest in her poems.

"Come, I know you've brought something."

"Yes. Yes, I did." She shuffled through the notebook in her lap. "Here's a nice short one."

"Let's hear it, then." He smiled at her, what was meant to be an encouraging smile but looked to Anita nothing short of rapacious.

"All right," she said. "It's called, 'The Maiden Aunt.' "

Not one I've seen, he thought. Another sonnet, dare I hope?

She began to read in a clear voice, less shy than he had expected it to be:

"She had in youth that thin grace boys pass by,
seeking a fuller breast or lip, a bolder eye.
The thought of going unloved lodged in her head.
Men came to meet her glance. Her glance was dead.

"It all seems now a silly, childish dream,
that ducks' eggs floating on the unfriendly stream
or apples, frozen on the leafless branch,
could ever have caused her pale, soft cheeks to blanch."

The thought of going unloved lodged in her head. Oh, dear, and she's so pretty! And a maiden aunt? Does that mean she has sisters, or brothers? Davis-Williams squirmed as the others bestirred themselves to comment, at last; for him, the poem seemed complete as it stood, and at The Body's question, why didn't she just slap on

52

some eyeshadow and buy a push-up bra, he almost leapt out of his chair.

They heard poems from others, some of them reasonably competent. He assigned a meditation: they were to write about their interrupting thoughts.

"This is the way the poet finds his material," he heard himself say, as he had said so often. "This is where the symbols that have power to evoke come from. The frozen apple on the leafless bough—a wonderful metaphor, wonderful. Resonates with all those other apples down through history, starting with the Garden of Eden, where the apple of knowledge was plucked, if you remember—"

"I'm not old enough," Sue Falk muttered. Miriam, jarred from the trance the poet's accent had induced, was conscious of an instant of blazing hatred.

"—The apples of Atalanta—" I'm losing them, he saw. "Well. Shall we begin? Twenty minutes, just sit quietly with eyes closed, inhale, exhale, and then begin writing down what came into your head. I'll tell you when the time is up."

They meditated. One of the older women fell asleep. They all wrote, including the sleepyhead. He discussed finding the form a poem wants to take. They wrote some more. And suddenly, it was after five o'clock. It hadn't been so very tiring, after all. He announced that he would give a reading of his own work at seven that evening in the room in which they had registered, assigned some overnight exercises, and dismissed the class. To his great disappointment, Anita Soderstrom emerged from the sliver of shade into which she'd crammed herself as the sun had swung around and headed straight across the rough lawn for the annex. Half his attention on the ones who wanted to speak to him after class, he watched her to the yellow door of her room in spite of himself.

*   *   *

Anita had lain down for a nap. She woke after half an hour and wrote in her journal for a time. The room was so quiet that she could hear a jay calling behind the building. "Solitude is the ultimate luxury," she wrote, and as the last word flowed from her pen someone entered the room next door and began bumping about; the television's inevitable rumble pounded through the wall.

Nearly time for Davis-Williams's reading, anyway. She put the notebook down on the bed and was just wrapping her flowered skirt back around her waist when the room door banged against the wall: she blinked against the flood of light.

Roz paused in the opening, glowering. Then she stepped into the room, slammed the door behind her, and leaned against it with her arms folded. "Well, Miss Prissy-Pants, I hope you're satisfied," she said.

Anita reached under her skirt and redistributed the cloth of her blouse around her waist. "How so?"

"How come you told the cops I went out last night?"

Anita moved to the mirror and pulled her hair back. "Didn't you tell them yourself?"

"You think I'm nuts? I told them I was here all night, from when we got in together." Roz looked without thinking into the other half of the glass, poked at a couple of curls that stood out farther than the rest, and turned automatically to check the side view.

"But you weren't. I heard the door close and I woke up and called you. Your bed was empty and you weren't in the bathroom."

"So?"

"Well, where did you go?"

"None of your business," Roz sulked.

Anita ran a comb into a twist of her hair and picked up the barrette that clipped back the ponytail. "In that case, can't you get him to give you an alibi, if you're worried the police will think you took what's-her-name's diamonds?''

"There wasn't any him." Roz dropped onto the end of her bed and ran one scarlet fingernail under the elasticized edge of her tube top, where it bit into her perfectly tanned breasts. "I went out to look at those stars some more."

"Oh." Anita smiled slightly as, in the mirror, Roz's lowered face assumed a scowl. So that was it. That was the trouble with images: sooner or later an honest impulse ran smack up against whatever you were pretending to be, and one way or another, something got damaged. "I'm sorry I told, then," she said.

"Sorry don't help, as Gramma used to say." Roz stood up and smoothed down her shorts, still white although she had been wearing them all day. "Don't you worry, Prissy-Pants. If I'm in trouble, my dad will make sure you get yours." She swept out of the room, slamming the door again as she went. Anita shook her head with the same small smile, picked up Roz's handbag from where the girl had dropped it, and quietly stepped out and shut the door. Ahead of her, Roz hustled up the smooth curb of the gravel path, her steps short and quick in the high sandals, a picture of outrage.

Anita followed more sedately. Behind her, the curtains on the unit next to theirs twitched and fell closed.

6

Roz snatched her purse without thanks and crossed the room to sit between Steve McCready and the Vietnam vet, a man with wild, light brown beard and hair and eyes that appeared dark until he lifted them to look at someone: then the clear pale blue, the color of the ice of a crevasse, made those who didn't know him stumble over their words. He went, for some inapparent reason, by the unmetaphoric name of Moose.

Anita found a seat in one of the extra chairs set around the edge of the room and waited, hands folded on the notebook in her lap, for Davis-Williams to appear. She was already stifling a yawn and wishing someone would open the windows to let the cigarette smoke out when he came in, holding a guitar by the neck, talking with his wife. The woman was instantly recognizable from Sue's description: entirely unfair. She did have roughly the same kind of face—there was the familiar wide, three-pointed smile—but it was softened and more feminine than Prince Charles could ever hope to be, even with the help of the best of makeup artists, and although the set of her head seemed as confident as any royalty, Anita thought she detected an underground of diffidence, or hesitancy, as if the confidence were . . . what was the word she wanted? Falsified? Counterfeit?

The poet pulled a tall stool forward and climbed onto it. From his place before the crowd he seemed to search the faces and find something wanting. "Well," he said. He smiled at his wife, who nodded. "This first one's set to music," he mumbled, picking at the strings of the guitar and fiddling with the tuning pegs.

The ballad he sang was his own, the tune an old Welsh one. His fingers were sure upon the strings, the chords true, his baritone as melodious as his heritage suggested. Alas, he'd followed ballad tradition by spinning out the tale until it seemed likely to break of its own weight.

Roz yawned with her mouth shut and gazed out the clerestory window beyond his head. The view was blocked by a large juniper bush. If she squinted, she could just see its blue berries.

The ballad went on. And on. Roz lit up a cigarette and examined Davis-Williams. She was quite sure a man could write poetry, maybe even attain a reputation equal to this man's, almost no matter what he looked like. At least she'd set her sights on someone with some superficial attractions: lean, not flabby, nothing in the slightest effeminate about him. *But they're all alike in bed,* she thought, with a grin that was almost spiteful. Her thoughts skittered to her father, straddled in front of the fireplace, beating time, Shall *I* com*pare* thee *to* a *sum*mer's *day? . . .*

The ballad drew to a lugubrious close with a prolonged minor-key flourish. Then the guitar was mercifully returned to its case and Davis-Williams began to read, short poems with far more to catch the ear. The audience stirred and settled into watchful quietness.

Now I've got them, Davis-Williams thought, puzzled at the failure of his ballad. What a bore. Now that he had something of a reputation, no one told him what went wrong anymore. He had to try things out in readings, examining the faces for glazed eyes and stretched nostrils . . . and where were all his students? He could see but fifteen of them, and surely anyone who had invested four hundred dollars in a workshop could be presumed to have some interest in the work of the instructor?

Perhaps, he mused, he could see enough of The Body to count her twice. She was wearing the same revealing top as when he'd first seen her, on the terrace that morning, the same pair of white shorts. The girl reached down to stub out her cigarette on the leg of her chair, and he found himself wondering if she would have been as flustered as he'd have been had her right breast popped out of the . . . could you call it a shirt? . . . as it had seemed about to do.

And now Doris had tilted her head to the left; time to stop reading. The wine and cheese were set out on a table at the other end of the room, as he had requested, and he was developing a certain yearning for wine and cheese himself. Or perhaps he wouldn't bother with the cheese.

7

THE ERSTWHILE AUDIENCE swooped like so many herring gulls upon the refreshments. If Davis-Williams had thought to hear some sort of comment upon his verse, he was disappointed. The talk was all of the burglary the night before, and of having been questioned by the police that day.

"It's an outside job, I hear," one portly woman in a pink dress was saying, as Davis-Williams edged past her. "Someone sneaked in—I hear there was another one like it at another resort a couple of weeks ago. They really should lock all the doors at night, don't you think?"

"Mmmm." The skinny, overly freckled woman Pink Dress had addressed swallowed a mouthful of cracker. "I heard it was one of the staff, and they're only trying to figure out who. My money's on that bus driver. I never did trust Indians."

"Not a guest, then?" asked a third woman. "I heard there was cocaine involved. And you know, those two really do dress kind of too rich, if you know what I mean. . . ."

Doris put her hand on her husband's sleeve, not just resting there but with the fabric pinched up between her fingers. "I do hope they don't think it could have been us?" she murmured into his ear. "Arriving so late . . ."

"Absurd," he said.

In her other hand she held a glass of wine, her square hand with its close-nipped nails, shortened for life with years of schoolgirl biting. He felt a flare of hatred for the hand. Not Doris, just the hand: and then recognized his pique for what it was. She might have got him some wine while she was about it.

"Are all your students here?" she demanded.

"Most of them." Does she think one's a thief? he wondered. He searched the room again, seeing Anita Soderstrom for the first time, talking to Dorothy La-Bruyere, whose gray head and pecking way of speech reminded him of a sparrow. "Those two over in the corner, and the ones I pointed out to you on the terrace this morning, and—"

"Including the Hot Tamale?" Doris interrupted.

He didn't even pretend to wonder whom she meant. "Alas, yes."

Doris gazed across the room at Roz, her lids half-lowered over her pale eyes. "To look at her, you'd think the only rhyme she could make without a dictionary would be monosyllables ending in -*uck*."

Buck, chuck, cluck, duck, began the tick in his brain. She should know that sort of woman doesn't attract me, he thought, his pique returning. "There's a surprising number of them," he said. "Twenty, I make it, counting the two you meant."

Doris pulled her chin back in satisfaction.

"It's true," he went on, musing half-aloud. "Sex seems her main interest. I can't quite make out why she's come. Certainly not to write poetry."

"Perhaps she'd have more interest in poetry if she hadn't outgrown her pants," Doris remarked, settling into what was becoming an all-too-familiar role.

"Perhaps," Davis-Williams agreed, losing interest.

"Oh, Professor!" said an elderly voice at his elbow. "I do want to thank you for your reading. I've wanted to say all day, what a wonderful accent you have. And such lovely poems! Not at all like that terrible stuff with all the profanity you read in these little magazines."

60

He turned gratefully to the woman, one of his students, and let the gush of her praise soothe his nettled spirit. Doris faded away. He couldn't blame her: even he found this sort of display distressing, and for her it was excruciating, although his fame was important to her. When he turned to look for her again, she was out of sight. Now, my turn, he told himself resolutely, and made for the wine.

Over the top of another conversation he saw his wife nodding in short, quick jerks at a young woman he didn't recognize. Little patches of color stood in her cheeks. What's she so angry about? he wondered: once he had collected a brimming glass of wine he drifted closer.

"I know just what you mean," the young woman was saying. "I could cheerfully strangle her! She's—oh!" She stopped and stared at him.

"You know my husband, of course," Doris said. "Carlotta McCready."

"Hello," Carlotta said. She juggled cheese on a cracker and an empty plastic glass to extend a hand. "My husband's in your class."

"Oh, Stephen, yes," he acknowledged, a shade uncomfortable. Stephen McCready was not, this time or any other, one of the better specimens.

"Seems the Hot Tamale won't let him alone," Doris said.

"Oh?"

"Cornered him at lunch today—poor Carlotta had to bring over an extra chair to sit with her own husband!"

Davis-Williams observed the girl curiously. She was a handsome creature, with vigorous features and a plaid shirt suitably taut over her breasts. Roundish dark-rimmed glasses gave her a look of quiet intelligence and blond hair rippled down to her jawline. Why should she worry? "I shouldn't take it personally, were I you," he advised. "She doesn't seem very, ah, well aimed."

"It's happened before." Carlotta frowned into her empty glass. "Excuse me. I need a refill, if there's any left." She slipped sideways into the crowd around the refreshments table, leaving Davis-Williams looking after her. In a moment she emerged with a full glass of red wine, lowered her head like a charging bull, and made for the corner where Anita Soderstrom was now talking to Stephen McCready. The next two weeks—twelve days, really—promised to be very interesting indeed, Davis-Williams thought as Carlotta inserted a lithe shoulder between her husband and the other young woman. He wondered what proportion of the interest would be in poetry.

But that was the distant future, and as a wave of fatigue washed over him he focused on the immediate future with far greater concern: "Doris," he asked. "Do you think we can decently get away for dinner now?"

Upstairs in the ladies' room, Anita opened the door of a cubicle to find Roz leaning against a sink, waiting for her. "Thanks for bringing my purse," she said. "I'm sorry I yelled at you."

"That's okay." Anita gave her hands a quick rinse and shook off most of the water. When her fingers found only an empty slot in the paper towel dispenser she blotted them on her skirt.

"No hard feelings?"

"No."

Roz dithered from one foot to the other and back. "Uh, what were you planning on doing tonight?" she asked.

"I thought I'd eat dinner, and then do the assignment for tomorrow."

"Uh, could I have the room for a while? Until, um, eleven, maybe?"

Anita raised an eyebrow at Roz, and then decided she didn't want to know. "I guess so."

"Thanks," Roz bubbled, giving her forearm a friendly squeeze. "All yours by eleven, I promise."

Anita watched Roz clip-clop down the stairs. If the dining room weren't too crowded, maybe she could work there. The band started tuning up over her head, and she hastily went down the stairs herself, before the ceiling over her head began its ominous creak.

At the door of the dining room she quietly took her place in line, notebook held demurely in two hands in front of her, and told the hostess she was a party of one. What an odd phrase: a party of one.

"Mind if I join you?"

Anita looked up from her notebook. "Oh, Moose, sure. Sit down."

Moose pulled out the chair opposite her and sat. "Crowded, isn't it?" he commented.

"Everybody wants to know about the burglary."

"Dummies. You'd think they'd be guarding their rooms," he remarked. "Are you starting or finishing?"

"Starting. I haven't even got a menu yet." The waitress appeared at that moment and poured coffee into Anita's upturned cup. Moose turned his own cup over and the waitress filled it and put the pot down on the table.

"Back in a minute," she said, darting toward the rack of menus near the cash register. Moose watched her go.

"You ever wonder what they think?" he asked. "I mean, what goes through her head when she's taking all these orders? The pay can't be great, and the food's pretty expensive."

"When it's this busy, a waitress doesn't have time to think," Anita said. "And they get the same food, free."

"You're kidding."

Anita shook her head. "I worked here one summer, a long time ago. Whatever's left at the end of the shift, they get, the waitresses and the kitchen help. Clean up the salad bar and so on."

"You worked here?" Moose looked again at the cedar-paneled walls, the blue calico curtains, the navy blue tablecloth with the blue and white checked paper napkins, and then across the table at her face.

"They've redecorated," she said. "But I bet it's still the same old boomerang Formica on the tabletops."

Moose picked up the edge of the tablecloth and checked the worn Formica. "You must know all these people, then."

"No. Everybody's gone from when I was here. Except for Jack Peletier, the bus driver, and I don't think he recognizes me. I was just a kid. Even the building's different—the annex is new, and they built on the Loft Bar since I saw the place last. And that must have been a long time ago, because whoever did it got some oak boards mixed in with the dance floor, and they're wearing out."

"Funny," Moose said. "I just can't see you sweating under a tray."

"Fair enough." Anita studied his face for a moment. Under the light brown beard and the shaggy brown halo, it was a fine-boned, almost delicate face, with a wide, expressive mouth nearly hidden beneath his mustache, and a long, thin nose with a tip that moved as he spoke. "I can't see you in Vietnam, either."

Moose squeezed his eyes shut. Red sparks. "Don't try."

"But that's what you're trying to write about, isn't it?"

A spasm of guilt gripped his face, but before he could answer the waitress reappeared. "Ready to order, folks?" she asked.

They placed identical orders for Salisbury steak, salad, and baked potato, the cheapest meal on the menu, and the waitress went away.

"How do you know I want to write about Nam?" Moose demanded.

"That's what you read about. In both the free exercises we did today."

Shocked that he'd given himself away so soon, Moose sucked his wide mouth into an oval and nodded slowly. "I don't know how, is the problem. It's a little like sex, you can write all the fuck and grunt you want, but you're not telling anybody anything. So they don't pay attention, even if maybe you've got something to say. And war is so—it's like they say, the worst obscenity, only it's worse than that, and better, and I don't know how to put in the—the rest—" Jaw thrust forward, he lined up the knife, fork, and spoon precisely one inch from the edge of the table, using the end joint of his thumb as a guide. "I don't know what I thought a nerd like Davis-Yumyum could do for me," he sighed.

"It can be done." She tilted her head at him. "Writing about war, I mean. Have you read Wilfred Owen?"

"Oh, him."

"It killed him, didn't it?"

Moose almost giggled. "Lady, that was a different war. Hell, it was a whole different *world!*"

"He's just as dead."

"He might as well have been writing about the red-coats lining up and all firing at once."

"The fear's the same."

"Is it? Is it?" Moose demanded, agitated. "What do you know about it? What could you possibly know about what it was like over there?"

"Nothing."

"I saw—what I saw—hell, I was just a *baby,* a baby right out of high school—what I saw, it comes back, you

65

know that? Only changed. You know that? In the night—"

"Moose—" Anita, white showing in her eyes, reached a hand across the table.

"Yeah, I know. Calm down. Shut up." He pressed his lips together and resisted the impulse to take her hand. After a moment he said, "I just want to be like I was before, is that so bad?"

"We can't any of us be that." Anita's voice came out thin and sad, and for several minutes neither of them said anything.

"What are they doing, growing that potato?" Moose asked suddenly, turning in his chair. He turned back. "I had a girl," he announced. "We were engaged."

"She didn't wait?"

"She waited." Moose readjusted the silverware. "She wanted to know, did I kill anybody. Hell, I'm *here*, aren't I? Of course I killed somebody. I dunno who."

Anita withdrew her hand and laced her fingers together in front of her.

"Yeah, that's what she did, too. She didn't want to marry somebody with *blood* on his hands. Not good enough for *her*. Oh, no, she had to have somebody *pure*—that's the word she used, pure, can you beat it? People like her, people like you, who weren't there, you can't know anything. Not a damn thing."

"That's why people like you have to tell the rest of us," Anita said, rather primly.

"Tell you! I'm just trying to put words to a scream," Moose exclaimed. Anita stiffened. "Okay," he said, with a sudden grin. "Let's back off. I don't know how I got started on this—Davis-Yumyum and his half-assed meditations, I guess. Let's just eat dinner and talk about this place."

The waitress arrived with their plates and set them down with a little flourish. Then she deposited a bowl of sour cream in the middle of the table, reached into her apron pocket and came up with a plastic bag of butter pats that she shook into a saucer. "Thanks," Moose said. The girl smiled and refilled their coffee cups.

"Everything all right here?" she asked.

"Fine, thanks," they said in unison.

Moose watched the waitress hurry away. "I wonder what she'd do if I said no?" he mused.

"She only wants to know about the food."

"That's about all anybody wants to know." He felt an old energy begin to pulse. Hate? Bitterness? Anger? Should he dare even try to focus it? He had a sudden impulse to turn tail and run, catch the next bus out of Coleridge to anywhere, jump into bed, and curl into a ball under the covers.

"The food is the only thing she can do anything about, that's all," Anita said calmly.

Moose stabbed his potato, squeezed the guts out, dressed the wound with sour cream. "They could do worse, I guess," he said.

His voice sounded almost normal. "About this place," Anita said, breathing again. Moose looked up and smiled, a square sort of smile that made her catch her breath before she continued, "I found some wild strawberries down one of the paths near the lake this morning."

His mouth relaxed. "You're kidding. Where?"

So, while the blood slowly returned to her head, she talked about wild strawberries, woodland flowers, and birds, and drew a map of the hiking trails on the table-cloth with her fingernail, and eventually dinner was done and she said she wanted to work on the next day's assignment and patted the notebook lying beside her.

"Here?"

"I'll have to. It's not even ten o'clock yet."

"What's that got to do with anything?"

"I can't go back to my room before eleven. My roommate has it, uh, tied up."

"Who's your roommate?" Moose asked, taking a swig of water in which the ice had long since melted.

"Rozlynne Haddad."

Moose choked and sputtered, his blue eyes bulging. "Shit, you sure can pick 'em," he managed to say.

"I didn't pick her. She was assigned." Anita balled up her paper napkin and tossed it onto the table. "Mostly she assigns herself."

"You know her?"

Moose grinned one-sidedly and shook his head. "Everybody knows our Rozlynne. In all senses of the word. She turns up at all the local poetry readings looking for Great Writers to take to bed. Though you'd be lucky if she remembered your name five minutes later. One of these days she's going to try on the wrong guy, and that will take care of that."

"You think so?"

I've frightened her again, Moose thought. How come I've frightened her, in a peaceful place like this? He leaned forward impulsively. "Let's do our homework together," he said.

She looked toward the door. "I don't know. They're still sort of busy," she said.

"Not here. In my room. I've got a single. We can roar out our lines at the tops of our voices and nobody will hear a word—"

She had sat back and was shaking her head, harder and harder, a crescendo of *no, no, no*.

Back off, Moose, boy, you're about to blow this one, he thought. "You don't understand," he started. "I really mean—"

"No. It's got nothing to do with you. *You* don't understand, because you can't," she said.

He sat back and looked at her for a few seconds, then

picked up his check, ducking the thin paper into his pocket so she wouldn't see it trembling in his hand. "Well, have fun," he mouthed. "I'll see you tomorrow." He mock-tipped a nonexistent hat. "Thanks, I think."

Anita watched him wind the path between the tables and pay for his dinner, the bump of her heart in her throat subsiding. She took a deep breath and opened her notebook and stared at it for a long time without seeing her own blue, upright words on the page before her.

8

HE HATED UNDERCURRENTS.

To be honest, he seldom understood these subtle, distracting alterations of tone of voice, these inexplicable hostile glances, or even the curious alterations of behavior toward himself that sometimes occurred. He regarded one and all as disruptive forces in the classroom. One great charm of the Summer Arts Conference was precisely that most of the students were strangers to one another, and the two weeks was too short to establish any serious liaisons or enmities among them.

In the past few days it had become apparent that this session was different. Davis-Williams sat in the soggy morning sunshine watching his students scribble. He'd given them a choice of three repeating forms, and it was obvious by the unfocused stares, the earlobes lengthened by anxious fingers tugging at earrings, and the readjustment of glasses on noses that most of them were having trouble coming up with rhymes. The Body wasn't even making a pretense: she had got up and wandered about thrusting her long tanned legs this way and that, as if modeling a bathing suit—and what she had on certainly covered less skin than the bathing suits Doris was accustomed to wearing. In films or magazines, such undress was titillating still; as he'd settled into middle age, seeing it in person evoked in him only a mild panicky distaste. A couple of the older women were clearly annoyed, if not by Roz's long lean legs then by her standing behind them to read what they were writing; they bent over their words and curled their wrists and forearms into walls around their notebook pages, but the girl seemed oblivious to this signal. He'd have to speak to her. A formless dread filled him at the prospect.

Anita Soderstrom, to contrast day with night, had placed her chair in the shade as usual, and was as usual prim almost to the point of being old-fashioned, a characteristic she accentuated by wearing skirts always. Even some of the old ladies wore shorts, revealing vast expanses of intricately varicosed thighs, but Anita, feminine as she was . . .

Was she that pale all over?

The lisping man, Saarinen, glanced at his watch and looked up at him, breaking his slide into daydream. Time, thank heaven. Friday morning. One week nearly done. "Time," he said, brightening his smile into rictus. "Well, how did that go?"

A chorus of groans.

"Oh, come, come!" He glanced over the group. Twenty faces, not one the least eager to read, most finding something of great interest in the paving stones. He read himself, instead, Dylan Thomas's great poem, "Do Not Go Gentle Into That Good Night," bringing himself almost to tears. Out of the tail of his eye he saw one of the blond beards crinkle the corners of his mouth in disgust. Screw you, he thought. See how you feel when you're fifty, your father dead without you there!

He finished the poem and regarded the group, who stared dully back at him like cows in a hot field. "I know it's somewhat early," he said, "but shall we break for lunch?" A murmur of approbation. "Two-thirty, then, and in the lounge this time, I think. They've got the air-conditioning working, at last."

Doris had gone with Judith Ammans—odd, how that acquaintance had blossomed—into Coleridge to buy some stamps and mail a letter to her mother in Leeds. They'd lunch at Gracie's, no doubt, a better place to eat than it appeared, so Davis-Williams decided to pick up a sandwich and take it to his room to look over some of the assignments that had been handed in. He settled for ham and Swiss cheese when the dining room proved out of roast beef and carried the sandwich up the stairs with a sense of profound disappointment. What was that line of Fielding's? *Oh, the roast beef of Old England!* No, not quite right, but he couldn't think how it was wrong and abandoned the line when he walked into the room and found that Doris had left the window open. He slammed it shut and gave the knob of the air conditioner a wrench, his teeth clenched. The heat might just drive him mad.

Or the poems. Boring, boring. Boring. The Body had turned in only a note of so personal a nature that he flushed and wanted to crumple it up. Instead, he scrawled across it, "Rhyme scheme? Scansion? and slapped it down on the pile of poems he had already read. Annoying creature. She had a habit of running her tongue around her lips, leaving them wet and shining with spit, that made him want to offer her a napkin, and he'd heard rumors about where she spent her nights— not that it was any of his business—and it did leave Anita alone . . . not that that was any of his business, either.

The sun had left his window screen, and instead of the golden haze that was all he could see in the mornings, the wooded rise behind the lodge stood as if listening for his step. Ridiculous, to sit here surrounded by all the *facilities* prettified in the pages of Seven Slopes Lodge & Resort's brochure, and remain in a still-warm room scratching old mosquito bites and reading bad poetry. He'd take a walk, leave these bits of doggerel to gather dust another day. Sunday, Sunday he'd finish them up, when there was no class.

Heartened by the prospect of playing hooky, Davis-Williams clattered down the steps to the middle floor of the lodge and pushed through the door into the parking lot. Which trail should it be? The sight of a healthy-looking man leading three noisy offspring up the hill reminded him that the warming house was full of potters hard at work; he made for the wooded trail that led eventually to the lake instead. Separated from the rough lawn by a solid hundred feet of aspens and red maples and an occasional fir, the trail was greenly shaded, with side trails that gave onto the lawn at intervals should he change his mind and decide to chance the sun and the bees.

The light, irregular shade of the woods was cooler than the sunny lot around the lodge, but no less humid. Davis-Williams followed the broad path laid out in bark chips with the springy step of a sauntering dog. He was too honest with himself, he liked to think, not to recognize that his eagerness was due in part to not having to listen to his wife identifying all the vegetation, whose names, whose real names, not the Latin specimen-jar names Doris insisted upon, he knew perfectly well himself. The resort had laid down a smudge against the bugs that morning, he remembered noticing from the terrace as his students pursued their rhymes: a good thing, too, because he'd forgotten his insect repellent.

The sweetish odor of sun lotion on the barely moving air warned him that someone was ahead of him on the trail. He therefore dawdled. A dragonfly hovered at chest height in a scrap of sun, its wings a transparent cloud. *Deep in the* something something *the dragonfly/Hangs like a blue thread loosened from the sky* . . .

Bladder campion and bracken grew mixed at the edge of the woods. A spray of raspberry in flower lifted his heart: in another month and a half, when the workshops were over, he could go and collect a pint of blackcaps,

buy a carton of heavy cream from the shop in town . . .
daydreaming of raspberries, still he took note of the
white stars of ground dogwood, the watery whisper of
the aspens. Ah, beautiful! He should make a poem . . .
one with a good, watery-sounding refrain. "The water-
wash of wind through aspen leaves." Not too bad, he
thought. A villanelle?

He rounded a turn in the path and saw, just ahead of
him, Anita Soderstrom standing stock-still. Her head was
dropped back, and he followed the line of her gaze: a
pileated woodpecker pocked at a dead maple limb in its
desultory way, high up where the canopy of leaves
began. Just below the woodpecker's branch had grown
another, torn away perhaps by winter snow leaving a
long rent, a scar filled with long, loose fibers that showed
that trees have heartstrings, too . . . a brief pain at the
thought made him wince.

Anita turned as the bark chips shifted under his weight.
"Oh, hello," she said. "I was watching the woodpecker."

"So I see."

Again she raised her face to the bird. Bits of punky
wood rained onto the path. She wore a knit shirt with a
high, round neck and short sleeves, and the flowered
wraparound skirt that had caught open on a terrace chair
earlier in the week and afforded him a glimpse of, alas,
only a petticoat. Somewhere she had picked one of the
wild roses that bejeweled the verge of the wood, and was
twirling it absently in her long fingers. "Do you mind if I
walk with you?" he asked, when the bird at last flew.

"Not at all."

He clasped his hands behind his back. "Uncommonly
fine weather we've been having," he said, feeling the
dolt he sounded.

She glanced upward, at the flecks of blue that could be

seen among the leaves. "I wish it would rain, actually. I miss the smell of wet woods."

"Ah." That marvelous fecund odor, yes. He felt he'd committed a gaffe; somewhat baffled, he examined the bark chips before him as he strolled beside her. What to say next? "Do you walk here often?" he asked. Wrong, wrong! What must she think?

"Every day." She sounded quite neutral, quite unoffended. "I usually skip lunch so I have time to think over the morning session."

"You think it over, do you?"

"Of course."

A twinge of conscience slowed his step. They did pay to come, he reminded himself. Quite a lot, even without adding in the lodging. They had a right to expect the best that he could give for their money, and here he was, escaping their doggerel instead of attempting some sort of constructive, informative comment.

"How did you come to write poetry?" he asked.

Anita shrugged. "I'm not sure. I've been doing it a long time, not with much success."

"You write very well."

She tilted her head a little sideways, as if she didn't know whether to take him seriously.

"No, really. You have an excellent ear."

"It's nice of you to say so," she said. "That's more than anyone's said to me in the past ten years, about my poems."

The pang of conscience then almost stopped him in his tracks. And there was more . . . what was he thinking? What was the matter with his heart? It seemed to be fluttering, a robin trapped in his chest.

"Why do you write?" she asked.

"Oh, I think, because of words." That was better: speaking calmed him. "I like words. Names. Just in and of themselves, the sound of them. Like, say, *Isphahan.*

It's a dirty little city in a backward country, no doubt, but its name turns it into moonlit marble."

She smiled. "Like Xanadu."

"Exactly," he agreed, although he thought of Xanadu as golden.

"I like words, too," she remarked. "I want to know where they come from, how they've changed. Like *sky*. It's straight from Old Norse, but it meant cloud—it got turned around a hundred and eighty degrees, somehow! And how do you get, say from *father* to *dad?*"

Davis-Williams laughed. "As it happens, that's easy. You've asked the right man, my dear! Dad's a Welsh word. It means, 'his father.' The word for father is *tad.*"

"As in tadpole?"

The first real, joyful grin of the summer, he thought wispily, as he felt his cheeks harden. "I think that tad's a toad. Anyway, in Welsh, father is *tad,* and it's my *nhad,* her *thad,* and his *dad.*"

"A different word for each?"

"That's right."

"Why?"

He'd never wondered. He shrugged. "Welsh is like that."

She scuffed along at the bark chips for several seconds. She, too, had clasped her hands behind her back as she walked, he saw, and her chin was thrust forward in the way he did himself. Could he take this as a sign of his influence? In his brash youth . . . "That's interesting," she said. "Is all of Welsh like that?"

He blinked, brought the conversation back to mind with a jolt. "Oh, yes. Here's another Welsh word. *Bardd.*" He grinned sideways at her. "Can you guess what it is?"

"Poet."

"Right. Only there are two of us, so we are *beirdd.*" He chuckled out of pure happiness. So long since he'd talked with a woman like this, just talked, not played games—Doris didn't care two pins—

He clamped down on the thought and stole another glance at Anita. Her hands were still locked behind her, her shoulders relaxed forward so that the soft cloth of her shirt lay close upon her breasts, clung there in the sultry air. The outline of her brassiere beneath the cloth was unaccountably exciting. A flash of memory from yesterday, or the day before: The Body reading something she had copied somewhere, lingering over the word *naked*. Himself thinking, she might as well be. That's it, he thought. That's what's the matter with me and Doris, she's lost her hold on my imagination: this insight he pushed away, and looked back at his companion. She had cocked her head to one side and he could see that she was trying the unfamiliar words silently upon her tongue.

A light sprinkling of freckles had appeared on her face over the past few days, making her pale skin seem even more lit from within. She's lovely, he thought, lovely, lovely. But I can't tell her, not even in Welsh. She'd guess what I meant. Or she'd guess I meant more than that, and perhaps I do. . . .

Just ahead, if he remembered rightly, a few yards past this next bend of the path, was a bench made of half a log split from a huge tree, with a carefully maintained view through the trees to the lake. Beyond that, the path branched, the wider branch leading along the lake and the other farther back into the woods to become a narrow trail, edged in muck and horsetails, that wound eventually to the lodge. He wanted to hold, to hold . . . *for deathless dower, this close-companioned, inarticulate hour* . . . Rossetti again!

Should he—did he dare—suggest that they rest on that bench, and then walk back the long, less-traveled way?

Before he could make up his mind, they had rounded

the bend. A teenaged boy hunched at the edge of the path, doing something that flashed in the dappled sunlight. Davis-Williams heard a stifled *oh!* from Anita: like her, he stared at the youth's hands, his red hands.

The boy, an Indian, jumped to his feet, gathering up whatever he'd been working at—blood! Blood! He had a dead rabbit, half its skin dangling from its red, naked body. "Here, you," Davis-Williams called, speeding up. "What are you up to?"

Rabbit in hand, the boy ran. Davis-Williams took several jogs after him but could see it was no use: the boy was already far ahead and running with the ease of youth and good condition. And he had a knife. Davis-Williams stopped with four heavy, flat-footed steps and went back to Anita, who still stood where he had left her, bent over something beside the path. "A poacher," he said.

She turned her head from her contemplation of the small pile of offal that lay in a shallow hole at the side of the path. "I thought small game wasn't in season until September?" she said.

He hadn't the foggiest notion. "I don't suppose it matters to that sort," he said. "Don't let it upset you."

She smiled faintly. "I'm not upset," she said. "My brothers hunt. He must have snared it, don't you think? I didn't hear a shot, did you?" Canting her foot on its side, she used the sole of her sandal to sweep the loose dirt into the hole and tamp it down over the rabbit's pathetic remains.

So she did have brothers. "A fitting burial," Davis-Williams said, feeling inane.

She glanced at the mauve-pink flower, which she still held, wilted though it was. "I think this lovely rose is gone," she said, echoing his own thought. He could feel his heart pulsing again. She cast the blossom onto the little grave and turned back the way they had come. "I think I'll go back and have lunch after all."

"Right." They set off toward the lodge at double the pace they'd been walking. And so the spell is broken, Davis-Williams thought. Or is it? He glanced surreptitiously at Anita's calm face, admiring her matter-of-fact ease. Most other women would be having hysterics, he imagined.

"That kid had bare hands," she said, as they took one of the paths that would lead to the lawn, and the terrace. "I hope he doesn't get rabbit fever."

A possibility he hadn't remotely considered. How like her, how like her poems, to show him another facet of the situation, beyond the facile sympathy for a furry beast! The boy's jeans had been faded, his shirt torn at the back, his black hair shaggy. The rabbit might be dinner. And after all, hadn't he just eaten of pig himself, having been denied his desire to eat of cow? Depending on others to keep the blood from view? Was not the boy then the more honest? He ticketed the thought to write into his journal at the first chance.

As they walked, a tingle started along the veins of Davis-Williams's arms, a tingle he recognized as he might the years-unheard song of a linnet. I'm falling in love with her, he thought. Me! Falling in love, I am, I am!

Not trusting his voice, he said nothing while they broke from the woods and swished through the longish grass and the clover with its humming hordes. A flight of small yellow birds twittered up from the lawn; he watched Anita's gaze follow their arc across the bare sky. The goddess Rhiannon, whose magic birds bring the dead to life, he thought.

"Are you going to eat?" she asked, before he could follow the notion to its root.

"I've had a sandwich."

"Oh. Then I'll see you in class. I'll go in through the terrace."

"I'll come that way, too," he said. "It's shortest."

Dazed as he was, he noticed The Body gazing at them from a chair on the flagstones, mouth drawn into a mocking smile that made him want to punch her for no reason at all. Your own guilt, you crazy old fool, he diagnosed.

The Body did her eyebrow-arching, shoulder-tossing trick. "Where've you been?" she asked.

"On the path to the lake," Anita replied. The words, to Davis-Williams's ear, were somewhat clipped. More undercurrents.

"Doing what?" The Body demanded. "Discussing Dylan Thomas?"

To his surprise, Anita turned pink. "No," she said.

The force that through the green fuse drives the flower, he thought. Then, with an intuition so sure it startled him, he realized that as usual The Body had it all wrong, she'd meant Lawrence, not Thomas, and that he and Anita had made love in the woods. I'm no Mellors, he protested in angry silence. He felt contaminated.

He opened the door to the dining room for Anita and was surprised when she instead stepped back.

"Owen!" Doris exclaimed as she came through the door. "I'd thought you must have lunched ages ago!"

9

EVEN IN THE air-conditioned lounge, one could sense the afternoon getting hotter and stickier. The sky turned milky with heat, and from the west-facing windows what seemed to be the outriggers of a storm could be seen approaching, curdled lines of cloud like seeds in furrows. Toward four o'clock, tall white cumulus clouds mounded on the horizon beyond the lake and slowly towered over the lodge, but they soon broke up without rain, without relieving the damp heat of the day.

The class was even more spiritless than usual. Davis-Williams called an early halt and told them to go write a sonnet out of the materials their prose exercises had revealed that afternoon, to be handed in on Monday. "Sonnet!" muttered the hairy one called Moose.

"Yes, sonnet," Davis-Williams snapped, feeling that the effort had cost him the last of his energy.

Dinner was likewise a dispirited affair. To add to his irritation, The Body sat at the next table and stared at him throughout, so that he skipped his after-dinner coffee and almost dragged Doris up to the bar for a drink. The Body soon appeared there, too. What could the child want?

"Why don't you take me to Bemidji tomorrow, to dinner?" Doris suggested. "Since there's no class on Sunday?"

"Bemidji!"

"We could look at the statue of Paul Bunyan and his large blue bull."

"Doris, are you quite all right?" he inquired, leaning across the table.

"Quite."

Now what? Bemidji! This session, Davis-Williams thought grumpily, was going wrong, wrong, wrong. He looked about him. The Body had moved and was again staring at him, with a curious expression he couldn't fathom. Doris followed his glance.

"I suppose it's a form of hero-worship," she said. "You must be something of a father figure to her." A scrap of conversation overheard earlier that week came back to him. One of the older women in the class: *I don't think it's sex, myself.* Gert Eylmar, that had been. And the grandmotherly woman, Dorothy LaBruyere, replying: *But if she just wants to be outrageous, she could shave her head and put a safety pin through her nose. Much simpler.*

And safer, Gert Eylmar had agreed. They had been speaking of The Body, he now realized, and of her scanty dress and pouting red lips. Well, then, what was the girl doing?

The miscellaneous twangs and thumps at the other end of the room paused. Someone said, "Two," and the music broke out, a series of shocks in his belly. The Steve creature evidently asked The Body to dance. He watched her lead the way through the blue light of the bar to the scrap of dance floor, glancing at Steve and then at himself, hitching her shoulder as if to say, why not you?

"Let's go," he shouted at Doris.

"I was just beginning to enjoy myself."

"Stay, then. I'm going back to our room and read."

"Oh, all right." She picked up her handbag and stood. The chair vibrated visibly as it scooted backward; were it not for the band threatening to blast everyone's brains out, the harsh scrape of the chair legs on the floor would have served as her exclamation mark. He knew the signs: a sullen evening ahead. In twenty-seven years, he had yet to discover what to do about it.

Even after a cold shower, he felt as if he had been dipped in melted ice cream and set out to dry to a fly-paper stickiness. Doris had changed while he was in the bathroom, into a pink, diaphanous nightgown. As he emerged into the room, she smilingly unpinned her hair and let it fall past her shoulders. In other times, in other rooms, the gesture had roused him to breathless desire. Tonight he simply regarded her with anxious wariness.

The telephone rang.

"Leave it," she said.

"It will just go on forever if I do," he said, and picked it up. "Yes?"

"Where's your wife sleeping?" someone whispered.

"Wrong room," he said into the phone, and hung up.

Doris seemed to shake herself. "Well, Owen?" she asked, coming toward him with arms outstretched.

"Well?" he countered.

Doris let her arms drop. "You are wearing out early, aren't you?"

"Doris." He sat heavily on the edge of the bed. "If you could find it in your heart to be just a bit less British, and close the window against the so-called fresh air and turn on the air conditioner in the sensible American way, perhaps I could find some remnant of energy to oppose to this infernal heat."

"Absurd," she sniffed. "You've lived here years and years, you should be used to it by now, just as I am."

"Who could get used to this, other than a Hottentot?" he protested, and fell back onto the bed without taking down the coverlet. "It's like a sauna. No wonder so many Finns migrated here."

Doris switched out the lamp and flung the curtains

wide upon a sky in which only the brightest stars hung like plump fruit. He steeled himself. She hurtled across the room in the dimness and flung herself on top of him, kissing wildly. He could try pretending she was someone else; that sometimes helped, but not tonight, he hadn't the energy. It was too damned hot and her limp flesh too damned familiar. Two old kippers side by side. He felt only a profound lack of interest.

Doris rolled off and stretched out beside him. "If you had the Hot Tamale in your bed, you wouldn't have any trouble."

"Even she wouldn't help."

"Even she!"

"It's this horrid heat, Dee. Can't we put the air-conditioning on, at least?"

"That's right. Blame it all on me."

He lay on his back, watching the pattern of light on the ceiling resolve itself as his eyes became accustomed to the dark. If that was the way she wanted to look at it, so be it. He was no Mellors. He stifled a short bark of laughter.

"What's so funny?"

"Nothing."

"You're thinking of the Hot Tamale. How she flaunts herself."

He sighed into the dark. "She may as well flaunt it while she's got it. She'll be a tub of lard by the time she's thirty. That sort always is."

Beside him, Doris shifted, but he got no sense of the purr he had expected. What would Lawrence have thought of this scene? he wondered. Or Thomas, for that matter? Ah, the lusty Welshman, couched with his some-what tattered bride! He reached for Doris's sweaty hand in the dark and squeezed it. "When the weather breaks," he promised.

At his first, sharp snore, Doris retrieved her hand.

Almost a relief, that he had been incapable: what she had felt in response to his evident fascination with that slut had been more desperation than desire; her dryness would have given her away. She began to lull her pounding heart by calling up the image of the room and naming all the things in it. Door, without panels: slab door. Doorknob, with keyhole: locking passage set. Frame of the door, comprised of jambs and lintel.

A tear mingled with the sweat on one cheek, but it carried no emotion with it, other than a vast weariness. On the brink of sleep she thought: In a way, I am more a poet than Owen. I at least still believe in the magical power of names.

Saturday morning.

Doris was first up, as usual. The air had cooled overnight without losing any of its moisture; as Davis-Williams feigned sleep to avoid any possible confrontation with his wife, he had the ridiculous impression that tiny drops of condensation beaded his flesh. The birds sang lustily—dreadful word to spring to mind, under the circumstances—in the woods on the hill behind the lodge. To keep his face still, he tried to identify as many as he could: there was a vireo, probably, chortling away like a soprano robin, and the burble of an oriole. That cut-time single-noted *clip-clip-clip* had to be a chipping sparrow. *Mi-so-so-so-so* sang a throat whose plaintive tune he knew but whose name he could not remember, and then came the creak of the other bed as Doris sat on the edge to put her shoes on.

What on earth was taking her so long? Pinning her hair? Hadn't she done that already?

The room door opened. "You can come out now, Owen," Doris said. The door shut. He felt her absence from the room like a breeze.

Relieved, he bounced up and ran his electric razor over

his cheeks to define his beard, washed quickly and dressed in shorts, sandals, and an old embroidered shirt with the collar button missing, and went down to breakfast.

Doris had already been served. He sat down murmuring apologies for sleeping so late, to keep up the farce. It didn't matter that she had seen through it; what mattered was to behave as if she hadn't.

In public, Doris had no choice but to go along. "What's on the agenda this morning, Owen?" she asked. She poked at the yolk of her egg as if she expected it to poke back.

"Arts Understanding Day," he sighed. Damn. He couldn't remember whether he'd reminded his class or not.

"Such gloom!" The egg yielded to Doris's fork and she deigned to eat a bit. "As bad as that, is it?"

Davis-Williams accepted a cup of coffee from the waitress and peeled back the top of one of the little cups of cream sweating in a dish in the center of the table. "Worse," he said to his wife. To the waitress he said, "Two slices of whole wheat toast, please, and whatever the fruit is today."

"Pots, is it?" Doris asked.

She knew perfectly well it was pots; she'd been talking to Martin Jonas from time to time all week, but he only nodded, watching the waitress head for the kitchen in her slender blue plaid dress. "Yes. We'll go over to the ceramics studio and be told how to make a pot, and when neither poets nor potters can stand the boredom any longer, we'll come back and everyone can go about his business." He finished off his coffee and inspected the sludge in the bottom of the cup morosely. "I suppose the coffeepot's empty?"

"You know I had tea."

Point to Doris. He tried the coffeepot and got a reluctant stream to fill his cup.

"I'll come along, shall I?" Doris announced. "I always like to watch the potters at work. I do hope they'll be at their wheels. It's rather like watching horses race, isn't it?"

"Mmmm." Davis-Williams wondered what possible connection horses could have with porcelain, and whether drinking the thin coffee was worth the effort. Deciding against it, he spread the paper napkin on his lap and looked for the waitress. "Come along if you want," he said. "I'm sure it's all the same to them, and I don't mind."

"No?"

"No," he said firmly, accepting his toast from the waitress. "And the fruit?"

"Cantaloupe," the waitress said. "In just a minute."

The melon was worth waiting for. It came with its scooped-out center filled with what must be the season's very first red raspberries. Davis-Williams sugared it contentedly, without even a grimace at having to use one of those annoying little paper packets.

"They say this heat will last until the middle of next week, at the very least," Doris remarked.

He hesitated, and took up the challenge. "Perhaps you'll become a convert to air-conditioning before then." A safe countermove. He dug a spoon into the melon.

"That toast looks good."

"Take it. This will be plenty for me." Doris waited a moment before reaching for the toast: breaking his fast on melon alone, when she had had two eggs and a piece of toast and sugar in her tea, gained him quite a few points. He finished the melon and tossed his scrunched-up napkin onto the table. Doris took the other piece of toast.

"Are you going up?" she asked.

"I must, if I'm to write in my journal. Must set a good example for my students, and I suppose it's only right to read some of the bits they've perpetrated." He smiled kindly: this put the room off-limits to her.

Doris nodded and went to work on one of the little plastic pouches of jelly with her teeth. It resisted her efforts, as always, and she looked up at him with her faded blue eyes wide.

"Give it here, and I'll have a go," he sighed. He pulled at the notch the printed red arrow pointed to, and the top of the pouch came off. He handed it over. Doris could perfectly well do it herself, he thought, irked both by her mute asking and by her lack of thanks.

By more than that. Climbing the stairs, he realized that somehow with that packet of jelly she'd come out on top in their game, yet again.

The Wednesday morning before, Roz had gleefully produced an electric coffeepot she had somehow acquired over Tuesday night. Older than she was, the thing had pretensions of grandeur: its battered shape was that of Georgian silver; its Bakelite handle scored to imitate carved wood.

It was as asthmatic as it was old. Roz had plugged it in with a giggle. "Wait'll you hear this," she said. The pot sighed and burped.

"That's almost obscene," Anita commented.

"No, wait, listen," Roz demanded. "It gets better."

The pot sighed again, burped again. The next sigh came at a shorter interval, and then the pot began burbling in earnest, faster and faster, until it ran at a continuous boil for a few seconds, clicked, and sighed long and heavily. "Just like the guy that gave it to me," Roz laughed, in her sunny morning mood.

The coffee turned out surprisingly good, like the dinner a martyred mother produces after long complaint. By Saturday a flying trip into Coleridge with Peletier in the pink bus had provided an even more elaborate breakfast: doughnuts from the general store, a little crusty with age beneath the powdered sugar, fresh nectarines (rather crisp so early in the season), and whitener in the coffee.

"That was good," Anita said, pulling the door of the room shut behind her. "I'm glad you got that pot."

"It has to go back tomorrow," Roz reminded her sadly. "Speaking of pots, isn't this the day we go up the hill?"

"I think so."

They struck off across the grass, Roz taking short steps to keep her ankles straight in the high-heeled sandals, yellow ones today, and Anita strolling slowly in her flat shoes. The lawn was still in partial shade from the lodge, the bees mostly absent, the clover-heads lying down in the heavy dew. "Have a good time in the woods with our Owen yesterday?" Roz inquired.

"He wasn't quite as boring as he can be in class."

Roz missed the sarcasm. "I guess," she laughed.

"All we did was talk," Anita said. "An ordinary polite semi-dull conversation."

"Oh?"

"It isn't me that's after him."

Roz placed her feet carefully to avoid a taller patch of grass. "I'm about to give up," she confided. "Unless maybe I can get somewhere this weekend."

"Good luck," Anita said. "Though I have my doubts."

They neared the terrace, where a few people still sat at breakfast. "What did you talk about, that wasn't boring?" Roz asked. "Just for some ammunition."

"Welsh words."

"Ick."

"Then we saw a boy with a rabbit, and our Owen got all upset, so we came back."

"Over the boy?" Roz asked, eyebrows arched. "Maybe I won't bother."

"No, the rabbit," Anita explained. "It was dead."

Roz stopped. "A boy with a dead rabbit? He killed it, you mean? Somebody staying here?"

"No, just some kid. Probably somebody who lives around here."

"Did you tell the guy at the desk?"

Anita shook her head. "Why should I?"

"Well, gee, a stranger? You remember what the cops said, if we saw anybody who didn't belong, we should say so?"

"Oh, that. I'd forgotten all about that."

"You can bet Mrs. Whatsit hasn't," Roz said. "I've heard more about her rings and her damn diamond bracelet than I ever wanted to hear about jewelry in my life."

Anita smiled. "If you say so."

"I mean it. If you didn't hole up in the room so much, you'd be sick to death of it, too."

They had started walking again, and Sue Falk flopped a hand at them from a chair on the terrace. She stretched her plump legs out in front of her and gave Roz the sort of look she usually got from men. "Well, well, well," she said. "Look who's here early. Still up, Rozzy?"

Anita glanced at her watch. Five of ten. "We are meeting here, aren't we?" she asked. "Before we go up to the ceramics studio?"

Davis-Williams appeared at the dining room door, saving Sue the bother of replying. "Here comes lover boy now," she said to Roz.

"Do your stuff, Haddad," Mim added.

Roz replied with a poisonous glance. "You two lezzies don't bother me," she said.

Whatever Mim had in mind to reply went unsaid: Davis-Williams came up to the table and began to apologize for forgetting to remind the class of Arts Understanding Day.

10

THE FULL CLASS had gathered by five past ten, Doris with them, and Davis-Williams led the group around the end of the lodge to pick up the path that led up the hill to the ceramics studio. The day was turning heavy already; one could almost see steam rise from the damp vegetation as the sun hit it, and the tar in the parking lot was already softening when they crossed it. The group straggled up the rutted path in twos and threes, looking totally frazzled despite the morning hour. Most of the poets, Davis-Williams thought, were as bored by this requisite "exchange of the arts" as the potters would be when the poets read their work to them, at the end of the coming week. He'd had eight years' experience, now, of how potters could glaze the eyes of poets, and vice versa.

Pleased with his pun (although it was scarcely the first time he'd thought of it) he chuckled as he strode unevenly on. He was still grinning as he pushed open the door to the studio, which served in winter as a warming house for cross-country skiers and snowmobilers—for all the ambition of its name, Seven Slopes could offer no downhill ski trails to interest any but the rankest novice.

The potting instructor, a man with wild, clay-gray hair and a walrus mustache, crossed the one large room to greet the poets.

Davis-Williams, waiting, wondered idly what the room looked like in winter. Now, shelves for pots in various stages of completion had been set up at one end. The moose head—where did all these lodges and chalets get so many moose heads, and what became of the other ends of the beasts?—over the bar had been covered with a plastic sheet to keep the clay dust off and the bar itself protected by a long tarpaulin. The gray wooden floor was uneven, worn by many boots. At the end opposite the shelves, several potting wheels had been set up, half a dozen of the hulking sort powered by the potter's feet, and five or six of the low-profile electric models. Past the shelves, a door led out to the kiln shed.

"Hi, Martin," Doris said, going to meet the ceramics instructor.

"Hi, Doris, hi, Owen." He grabbed both their hands at once. "Who'll do the tour, you or me?"

"You, of course," Davis-Williams said. "Do you want them all at once, or in batches?"

"All at once is fine," Martin replied. "Keep together, everyone," he instructed, raising his voice. "And don't get too close to the wheels—clay flies." He shepherded the poets into a crowd around one of his students, who had consented to demonstrate how to throw a pot. "All yours, Greg," he said to the student, and stepped out of the circle.

"Well, hello," Davis-Williams heard Martin say to someone behind him.

"I didn't realize you were the instructor," came Anita's light voice, drowned immediately in a chorus of *oohs* as the spinning clay became first an even mound, then a hollow cylinder, then, with what looked like the most minimal of motions, a bulging form with a narrow neck that was swiftly drawn higher.

"A weed jar," Doris said, almost clapping. "What a nice shape! Can I have it when it's done? Buy it, I mean, of course."

The potter looked down at the raw, wet clay, on which his fingers had left a creamy trail of slurry. "It may not come out very well," he said doubtfully, covering the quiet urgency of Martin's voice that Davis-Williams strained to hear. "Things happen to pots."

"Nonsense," Doris declared.

"Please," Davis-Williams heard Martin say, "Is it so much to ask? Is it?" and a soft *shhh* in reply. He tried to drift backward through the crowd, but instead was carried forward to the next wheel, where a student was throwing a lid to fit a tall jar standing on a board at his elbow.

"A well-fitted lid is a sign of good craftsmanship," the student said. "We always fire the lids in place on the jars, to prevent warpage in the kiln." Davis-Williams felt a definite tedious shifting among the poets behind him. Somewhere in the studio, that other conversation lilted and fell. The poets were directed on, to another potter standing ready near the tables where the clay was wedged. "Before throwing a pot, the clay must be made uniform and free of bubbles," this student intoned. Davis-Williams clamped his jaw on a reflexive yawn as he anticipated the demonstration forthcoming, which consisted in a lot of banging and slapping and kneading of the clay.

A crack like a shot echoed through the room.

"All right, you!" somebody screamed. He whirled to see Roz Haddad launch herself, bright fingernails first, at a young blond woman who had snatched up a white disk and held it before her as she backed away.

Only to gain room. The blonde—Carlotta Mc-Cready!—flung the disk at The Body. It missed her head by a fraction and shattered on the floor: plaster. Dear heaven!

"Here, you two," Davis-Williams said, making himself run toward the two women.

Stephen McCready grabbed his wife from behind and held her arms at her sides while she struggled. They lurched against the metal shelving and pots crashed to the floor. "Get her out of here," Carlotta shrieked. "Get her out, out, out!"

The potters converged on the scene. Roz was shouldered out of the way.

"I think you had best wait back at the lodge, Miss Haddad," Davis-Williams said. "You may be excused from this exercise."

"Oh, no you don't! Let me at her!"

He snatched at The Body's arm and held on, feeling his fingers dimple the soft flesh just below her armpit. "Miss Haddad!" he shouted.

"Let. Me. Go," she yelled through set teeth. She scratched at his hand with her long fingernails, and he tried to grab her around her body, arms prisoned at her sides, as McCready had done with his wife, but her arms got loose and somehow, he wasn't sure how, she had turned in his arms and flung her own around his neck and pressed her soft undulating torso against his, and began sobbing against him.

"Miss Haddad," he protested.

"That's enough," Doris said icily. She began to pry at The Body's arms, while Davis-Williams set the heels of his hands against her taut belly and tried to push her away.

Suddenly she loosened her grip.

"Okay, Rozzy, baby." The man called Moose had buried his fingers in The Body's hair. He tightened his fist. "Let's go back to the lodge and have a cup of coffee, right?" he said quietly.

"Okay," she sniffled.

Davis-Williams caught a glimpse of brown smears of makeup on her cheeks as she turned. She walked sedately enough, but Moose kept his hand buried in her hair and marched her out the door. The screen slammed behind them. Over by the toppled shelf, someone cried

95

softly, and he heard the chink of shards of dry clay being picked up.

"Well," he said to Martin. "I say! I must apologize. I had no notion what I was unleashing!"

Martin paid no attention beyond a backward wave of his hand. "How much is broken?" he asked.

He got some reply from a squatting student. Carlotta groaned. "I'm so sorry," she said.

"Most of it was yours," said the other student.

"I'm glad of that, anyway."

Martin turned back to the poets, standing helplessly in the somewhat clear center of the room. "Let's go look at the kiln," he said. "We're firing today. Unless someone else would like to throw a fit?"

Some uncomfortable shuffling. Davis-Williams bit back another apology. What could be done?

Martin led the group single file behind the shelves and through the outer door.

The heat of the kiln hit their faces even before they stepped under the roof that was its only protection from the weather. Even Davis-Williams, still sunk in proprietary embarrassment, felt a little pleasant excitement. The roar of the flames in the kiln mouth, the little tongues of fire escaping the peepholes—even in this weather, they had power to enthrall.

But there were no little tongues of fire escaping from the peepholes. Miriam, trust her, asked why not.

"You're thinking of a glaze firing." Martin seemed to slip with relief into his usual pedantry, although he glanced nervously toward the studio as he spoke. "We fire our glazes in a reducing atmosphere, that is to say, with an overall oxygen deficit—"

By the shifting of feet behind him, Davis-Williams knew the poets were again getting lost. Martin went on interminably about the chemistry of glazes, how the colors were controlled by the amount of oxygen available in the kiln as well as by the presence of certain metallic salts . . .

Doris's ears moved backward in a stifled yawn.

"It looks awfully hot," Sue Falk said.

"It's hot, all right." Martin grinned and rocked back on his heels. More lecture coming. "We're almost ready to stop the firing—just over a thousand degrees centigrade. That's almost nineteen hundred degrees Fahrenheit. And this is just a bisque fire."

The poets looked impressed, or perhaps only sleepy. "What's bisque?" Sue asked.

Martin picked up some broken pieces from the ground near the kiln. "We fire first to a soft, stable body," he explained. What was Moose doing with The Body? Davis-Williams wondered. His mind went haring off after the possibilities, and he sternly called it back. "That way we can apply glaze without worrying over whether the pot will get soft and fall apart," Martin said. "Here's what bisque looks like." The pieces were solemnly passed around. His ears crackled with boredom. Was someone raising his voice again, in the studio?

"But if you want to see real heat, come back when we're firing porcelain," Martin continued. "Gets up to thirteen-fifty degrees, then. Centigrade, of course. Fahrenheit, that's almost twenty-five hundred."

Somebody whistled. "What does that do to the pots?" one of the beards asked.

"Vitrifies 'em. Makes them into a kind of coarse glass, that is. Very durable. Unless a pot gets ground up, it or its pieces last literally forever."

"Is it stronger than metal?" somebody wanted to know.

"As far as heat goes. Most metals would be close to vaporized in there." Martin jerked his head at Sue Falk. "If you dropped your pretty ring in, all you'd find afterward would be a blackish little blob."

Sue hastily polished her silver ring on the back of her shorts and stuck her hand in her pocket.

"What would it do to a person?" the same beard wanted to know.

Martin's eyes drifted toward the studio door. "Oh, a person would be gone, ashes. That's what I threaten my students with, to keep their noses to their wheels."

"You mean, you could get rid of a body in there?" Mim exclaimed, incredulous. "Just stick it in with the pots and nobody would ever know?"

"Oh, dear Lord, no." Martin glanced again at the studio door. "It would wreck all the glazes. And there'd be ashes. Come and see the new kiln we're building."

The poets moved away from the hot shed, and the topic, with general relief. Even Davis-Williams could see that Martin was calming himself with his long, cadenced sentences about catenary arches and the orifices of gas jets, and he shifted from foot to foot without interrupting. At last the characteristics of fire brick had been explained in every detail, down to comparison with Space Shuttle tiles, and the visit could be adjourned.

"We'll meet in the lounge in twenty minutes," Davis-Williams told his crowd. His eyes roved over the faces: four missing. McCready would be with his wife, Moose and The Body having that cup of coffee or whatever, but where was Anita Soderstrom? "Off with you, now," he heard himself say, "and think poetic thoughts about pottery."

"Excuse me," Martin said. "I want to go see what the damage was."

Davis-Williams watched his colleague trudge up the slight incline to the studio, and then shuffled after his students. He could see them, a straggle like a group of Girl Guides leaving a zoo, through the trees. Little do they know, he thought, that they will have to write a poem about potting. In class, rhyme required. He smiled gently, the smile of a man whose practical joke is about to succeed.

Sue tramped into the lounge just ahead of Miriam and well ahead of anyone else, and more fell than sat into one of the couches. "I wish I knew what form he's planning to assign," she sighed. "Then I could get a head start."

"Oh, well." Miriam sat down and opened her notebook. "At least we can cook up a few rhymes before he gets here. How about splitting a seafood salad for lunch?"

"Are you thinking of lunch already?" Sue scribbled a couple of words in the margin of her notebook, rhymes she did *not* propose to share with anyone who could eat as much as she liked without putting on any weight! She paused. "Sounds good," she said. "Let's do that."

It was, as usual, a disappointing batch: he kept up the exercise only so that the potters could hear something about themselves in the final reading, now less than a week away. Davis-Williams sighed heavily. Much worse than usual, to be blunt. Probably because of The Body's little charade. There were, as usual, several that homed in on the transformation of the gooshy—odd, how that aggressively unpoetic word turned up, year after year—clay into rock-hard, permanent stuff. Only one, this go-round, rhapsodizing over potsherds on the fields of time. Two fire gods, one phoenix, and the inevitable joker who wrote an ode to *Cannabis sativa.* "Two n's in Cannabis," he scrawled across the top of the page. Doris, to whom a yellow primrose was *Primula vulgaris,* nothing more, would be proud of him. The grandmotherly lady had written about tea cozies, a welcome relief, although how she had gone from porcelain to patchwork remained mysterious. And then—

"Ah, here she is," Davis-Williams exclaimed *sotto voce*. He wished he could read the poem aloud. He glanced at the candle he had lit for his students to meditate upon, the flame as tall and still as if he had set it out on the terrace this still, close day. Never mind. He'd read it silently. "Narrow-Necked Jars," she'd called it.

> The hand, more sensitive
> than the eye, though slower,
> draws the clay's hollow tower
> into a neck so thin, no slip
> of water past its lip
> can help a single flower live.

Nice, that, he almost exclaimed, pleased by the one internal rhyme. Did she keep it up? No. Too bad.

> Fit only, by design, for straw,
> or for the sun-dried stalks
> of weeds gathered on walks
> through fields where autumn bares
> the beauty of the fenceline tares
> and lets us carry home our awe,
>
> Narrow-necked jars, honed
> on fire, and knowing all
> the power of flame, can call
> us to confront the plain,
> to unravel all the skein
> of lives we've knotted, and disowned.

Well. Well. He wasn't sure the use of *tares* was quite correct, and he'd certainly seen her do better, but imagine producing that in the space of fifteen minutes, without a dictionary! And with almost no crossing out! Though with much chewing of her pencil, he recalled tenderly, smiling as he turned to the next poem, another marijuana one that started, "On a sunny summer day/ We all went to see the clay."

Finished with his red marks, he turned back to Anita's poem. *Good,* he'd written across the top, and now he underlined the word for good measure and added a twin. What was the skein of lives she'd knotted, and disowned, poor maiden aunt? He found himself daydreaming again, of gently introducing her to her body, to his body. Horrified at the thought that he might start scribbling on the nearest bit of paper, sure to be one of the other students' poems (and in red ink!) he pulled himself up short. Time, past time to stop the candle meditation, have them read, and conclude class for the day. One week down, and one to go. He'd make it up to Doris in Bemidji this weekend, somehow.

"Time," he said. "Who'll read first?"

One of the beards began to read about the peachy fuzz of candle flames, and Davis-Williams lifted his eyes to the window. One small teasing cloud sat on the horizon. Would it never rain, and dispel this miserable, sticky weather?

11

DAVIS-WILLIAMS FOLLOWED HIS wife out of the dining room, trying to balance his notebooks and the two white boxes of sandwiches they planned to carry to the bench that overlooked the lake. Just outside the dining room door, a little way down the hall, he saw Anita Soderstrom backed against the wall. The man called Moose stood over her, leaning on one hand planted against the wall next to her head.

"I never said anything of the kind," he heard her say. Snipped words.

"Swear?" asked Moose.

He wanted to slow down, to hear the rest of the conversation, which struck him as vaguely ominous, but Doris was already at the double entrance doors motioning to him to hurry up. He glanced over his shoulder as he reached the doors himself, saw Moose standing upright, a half step back of where he had been, his hands poked into the pockets of his disreputable jeans. Perhaps whatever it was was all right, then.

"Come *on,* Owen," Doris insisted. He caught up with her as she started into the shade of the path he had walked with Anita the day before. As usual, she strode ahead while he tried to cope with the slipping notebooks and lunch boxes. *"Arisaema triphyllum,"* she declared loudly. *"Anemone canadensis!"*

"I know, I know," he muttered.

"When we come back, I'll gather some of that *Lychnis* and a few sprigs of *Aquilegia* for the room, shall I?"

"Lovely." He nodded at the pendant red and yellow flowers. *Columbine*, he thought. I know you. *Campion.* Why can't she talk like a person instead of a botanist? It's not as if she were teaching. The aspens and maples— *Populus* and *Acer* to Doris, he supposed—bright with sunlight above his head nevertheless seemed to brood. Doris plumped down on the bench at the bend of the path and held out both hands for the boxes. He handed them over thankfully and juggled his notebooks onto his lap as he sat. Framed by the carefully trimmed trees, a solitary water skier kicked a lacy plume out of the blue lake. For no reason he could fathom, the scene brought back quite another—the damp, musty-dusty smell of a punt on the Cherwell, years before. He'd steered through a family of swans, and the cob had flown at him, hissing, neck straight as a machine gun barrel, and given him a quite shockingly nasty nip on the elbow. . . . Doris stuffed the box strings into a pocket and handed him a sandwich. As he sank his teeth into it she began to question him about the people in his class. He took a perverse delight in the small black flies that crawled into his eyes and hers as she went on and on.

The whiteness of the plume of water, and its speed. That was what had brought the swan to mind . . . How tenderly Doris had bandaged his arm! A golden cloud of midges had danced over the punt. . . .

"I don't know anything about her," he found himself saying, for what seemed the hundredth time: this time about Dorothy LaBruyere. "She has short gray hair and stinks of roses. That's all."

"Can't you tell anything from her poems?"

He shrugged. "She reads. Otherwise, not much." Her poems. From her poems. Where had Anita been, during Martin's kiln speech? He couldn't picture her. Yet she must have been there, he thought, oddly shaken. She wrote that poem about the kiln fire.

"Owen?" Doris prompted.

"Sorry, Dee. I was distracted. What was it?"

"Oh, Owen, really! I asked you about that hairy brute with the wild blue eyes!"

Three more days of this damp heat and he'd not be shocked to find mushrooms growing out of his navel. And Doris would look them up in one book or another, no doubt. If she didn't have the right volume, her new friend, Judy whatever, was sure to.

"If she's having so much trouble hanging onto him, why bother?" Roz leaned back from the mirror and examined her side view.

Anita, sitting on the bed, opened her mouth with a small *tcch*. "Roz, they're married. She loves him."

"I wouldn't love a guy who didn't think twice about jumping into bed with somebody else," Roz said over her shoulder, to her own reflection.

Anita raised her hands and let them fall into her lap. "What's it to you, Roz?" she asked. "Can't you back off and give them a chance?"

"I like him. He's fun." Roz leaned toward the mirror and began to draw upon her pristine face with a brown makeup crayon; her left eye became instantly larger, more lustrous, and more mysterious than her right. She blended the makeup with her little finger. "I thought we were staying out of each other's business," she reminded Anita. "I stay out of yours, you stay out of mine. Isn't that what we said?"

Anita shrugged. "Are you giving up on Owen, then?" she asked.

"Uh-uh. My business." Roz did the other eye and deftly painted her lips with bright red. She grinned. "But try and make me, if you really want to know. I've got another card to play, now." She displayed the inside of her left arm. High up, three round bruises showed through her tan. "Look what he did to me."

"At the warming house?"

"Who's to say?" Roz smiled, her lips compressed.

"What about Steve McCready?"

"If you can't stay out of my business, don't expect me to stay out of yours," Roz said good-humoredly. She dropped the lipstick into her handbag and zipped it shut. "See you later."

Miriam Dubbins sat on the terrace with a glass of iced tea, earnestly consulting a rhyming dictionary that bore the gray evidence of use on the edges of its pages. She looked up and smiled vaguely as Anita came across the lawn and, to her relief, went into the lodge.

"I wonder why she always wears a skirt?" Sue Falk asked, looking down at her own brown knees, glossy with sun oil.

"Cooler than jeans, she says."

"You asked?"

"Mmm." Miriam gazed at the dictionary in despair. The only rhyme it gave for *kiln* was *Milne,* and what could she do with that? Pooh's honey pot, for Pete's sake?

"Why not just wear shorts?" Sue stretched to see what Mim was doing. "The potters say *kill.*"

"I know, but it looks funny," Mim said. "She sunburns real easy."

"Oh, is that why she's so pale? Damn. I was hoping she was just out of jail, or something."

Miriam decided to ignore the comment. "I see lots of rhymes for kill," she announced doubtfully.

Anita emerged from the dining room carrying a glass of something iced. She sat at a shady table and began to write steadily. "Look at her." Sue waved away a fly that had taken an interest in her sun oil. "Show-off. She doesn't even pretend to stop and think."

"Probably writing prose. Did you know there are sixty-four rhymes for *kill* and not one of them will do?"

"What do you s'pose she was doing in the woods with Owen yesterday?" Sue mused.

"Oh, stop it," Mim snapped. "Here, if you're not busy, get us some pop. My wallet's in my tote bag."

Late that afternoon, the Davis-Williamses passed through a thunderstorm consisting of two flashes of lightning, a couple of halfhearted rumbles, and a spatter of rain that left the pavement polka-dotted. "That's only going to make the humidity worse," Doris complained above the clatter of the old Chevy's fan. "I guess I'll need some air-conditioning when we get to Bemidji, after all."

Her husband, eyes on the yellow line down the center of the road, pretended not to hear.

Sunday dawned cooler than the last few days had been, but just as humid. The meteorologist on the orange television screen in the lobby of Seven Slopes Lodge excitedly predicted thunderstorms and cool weather for the middle of the coming week. Nobody was watching, however; not even Jack Peletier, who lounged in one of the fat leather chairs talking to the girl at the desk. "We should get those kids away from PacMan for a while, eh, Vivian?" he said. "Tour the garbage dumps in the bus tonight, eh? Maybe spot a bear."

"What do they care?" Vivian sniffed. "Bunch of spoiled brats. Only reason they're here is their parents are afraid to leave them home alone."

"Eh, a bear might do them some good."

"If you fed them to it, maybe."

"There's a big one comes around the warming house," Peletier said. "Saw its tracks, yesterday, day before."

Vivian clasped her hands on the counter and leaned her bosom on her forearms. "Speaking of the warming house," she said. "You know that slut with the Arts Conference? Did you hear what she did yesterday?"

Peletier listened, his wrinkled face impassive. "She's one, all right," he said, when Vivian had finished. "You know something else that happened yesterday?"

"No, what?"

"That Hanson kid took a deer, over to the end of the lake. Broad daylight, eh?"

"I guess that means we have to fix the fence again," Vivian complained. "I don't know why he can't just crawl under the wire like anybody else."

Peletier yawned. "No sense fixing it. It just comes down again."

"Comes of having those fancy wirecutters," Vivian said. Her nostrils widened. "I don't mind Hanson," she added, "but I hate strangers just running through the grounds whenever they damn please," she said. "After that burglary last week I don't feel safe at all anymore, I don't care what the sheriff says." The telephone rang. "Gives the place a bad name." She picked up the phone.

Peletier folded his hands on his thin midriff and let his dark eyes drift toward the television, where a black and white movie outlined in orange showed Indians creeping up the back side of a pile of rocks while the unsuspecting cavalry jingled along below. Ominous music drowned out all natural noise. Ought to be able to tell by the music things weren't right, eh, but for once a white man's invention seemed to be on the Indians' side. And where did they hide the orchestra? Eh? Down in that skimpy gully?

"They want the shuttle at Gracie's," Vivian said.

Peletier nodded and stood up. He shook his pants

pocket to be sure he had the keys to his steed, and went out to the parking lot.

*   *   *

By nine o'clock, because of the clouds, it was dusky enough to call dark. Anita, who had been lingering over dinner to talk to Dorothy LaBruyere and Dawn Atkins about the past week's class, cut across the lawn to the annex. The Do Not Disturb sign was hanging on the doorknob.

"Oh, hell," she sighed, and followed the path through the spruces back to the lodge. Roz must be returning the coffeepot. Double hell.

She settled in the downstairs lounge where classes were held, wishing she had something to read besides her own notebook. Lacking that, she ripped out one of the lined pages and began to write a letter.

At eleven-thirty, she went back to the desk and asked the clerk to buzz her room. "Just ask her if the coast is clear," she said. "I don't want to talk to her."

"No answer."

"Thanks."

Anita walked again through the hot dark to the room. The tag was gone. So was Roz.

The phone rang as she turned down her bed and pulled her nightgown out from under the pillow. "Do you know what your husband is doing?" whispered a low voice, she thought female, when she picked it up.

"Rotting," she said clearly, and hung up. Long after she had put on her nightdress and lain down, Anita stared at the dark ceiling, slowly stroking the bare fourth finger of her left hand.

12

"Is THAT YOUR good one, just coming in?" Doris asked. She lowered her eyes so that she shouldn't appear to be staring, and Davis-Williams turned round in his seat.

Anita Soderstrom, looking cool and more feminine than ever in a blue flowered dress, stood uncertainly in the doorway to the dining room, searching the tables but apparently not finding anyone she knew. "Yes, that's she," Davis-Williams said.

"Ask her to join us?"

"Well, yes, I think I may," he said, startled. The trip to Bemidji had been an unmitigated disaster, the drive back the night before in the heat trapped under clouds that subbornly refused to rain properly silent and sullen. Silent and sullen, in part because he had refused to accompany Doris to church now that he could no longer confess himself as a miserable offender and pray to be restored to a godly, righteous, and sober life: the new language offended him. Doris had no understanding of the importance of form, of the long history of phrases repeated generation upon generation.

"I should do so, then," she said tartly. "Before she leaves."

He got up and traced a winding path among the tables. "My wife and I wondered if you'd care to breakfast with us," he said to Anita.

"Oh! Yes, I would," she replied.

"We're by the window. You won't mind the sun?"

"No, no," she said. "I like the sun, really, and once it goes through glass it doesn't hurt."

He pointed out the table, with Doris sitting at it, her hair like brass in the sunlight Anita so studiously avoided. Nice, nice, that men were to let ladies go first, he thought, following the slim figure in the flowered dress. The better to enjoy the rear view.

"Good morning," Doris said, quite civilly.

"Good morning. How nice of you to think of me."

"Well," said Doris cheerily. "I saw you standing there like Orphan Annie, and I thought, that girl needs rescuing."

Anita smiled her other, thin-edged smile and sat down. Davis-Williams took the chair opposite, with a side glance for his wife. What on earth was she up to, now?

"Have you ordered yet?" Anita asked.

"Not yet." Davis-Williams picked up his menu. "Here, take this. I've got the bloody thing by heart."

While they waited, and while they ordered, and while they waited some more, Doris sharpened her tongue and began to prick. Davis-Williams sat his temper and let her go on, knowing her purpose was to make him seem an idiot but confident that Anita, who seemed quite able to hold her own in her quiet way, would see through to his wife's petty jealousy. It was often like this with a good student; her knowledge of botany was never enough for Doris; she wanted also to write well, poor dear.

Doris whittled away. He found it merely tiresome, as he had found so much tiresome these past few months. "Mid-life crisis," Doris called it, and tried to junk up his brain with pop psychology.

"There's Roz," Anita murmured.

Davis-Williams followed her gaze. The Body, wearing only a tight white shirt, exactly like the one he himself wore under his Mexican pullover, and a pair of blue shorts pared high enough to reveal the crease beneath

110

her buttocks, was just about to sit down with one of the other students. "Isn't that Saarinen?" he asked.

"Yes." Doris now stared at The Body and The Wimp with great interest.

"Where's his wife?" she asked.

"Gone back to St. Paul."

Davis-Williams digested this information as he contemplated the pair for a moment or two. "He's a fool," he said. A wave of jealousy passed through his belly: not of the man for having The Body, but of his having the opportunity . . . no, of his *making* the opportunity. . . .

"She's very attractive," Doris pointed out.

"So's his wife," he said, without thinking.

The waitress, the providential waitress, arrived before Doris could frame a retort and handed round the plates of food, mixing up his eggs and sausage with Doris's eggs and bacon. When that was straightened out, Doris put her hand on his wrist. "I suppose you live all alone," she said to Anita.

The waitress returned with the coffeepot as she spoke, and filled all the cups, even Doris's, which still had some tea in it.

"Where do you live, Anita?" Davis-Williams asked, when the unfortunate waitress had gone off to fetch another cup. "In Minneapolis, I mean."

"On Vincent, near forty-third."

"Vincent!" Davis-Williams's fork jerked against his plate and he put it down without eating anything. "In Linden Hills? Why, that's only three blocks from us! Do you mean to say that a poet as good as you has been living only three blocks from me, and I never knew?"

The rims of Anita's ears turned pink. She seemed unable to find a reply.

"You have a house?" Doris asked, after a sharp glance at her husband. "It seems to me that area's all single-family houses."

Anita let flash that other smile, the flicker of a minnow in a sunny stream. "No. The house is divided up. I live in the, um, garret."

"A poet in a garret on Vincent Avenue!" Davis-Williams exclaimed, his voice ringing with dazed pleasure. "Marvelous! I didn't know they built garrets in this country."

"Attic, then."

"Could I have the salt, please?" Doris asked.

Anita passed the salt across the table. "It's a very nice attic, really," she said. "It's got outside stairs, so my comings and goings don't bother the family downstairs, and I've got a little porch where I can grow a pot of tomatoes."

The possibilities of the outside staircase hit Davis-Williams with almost hallucinatory force: Anita in a soft, velvety, deep-red dressing gown, the sort that wraps and ties at the waist in a single, easily loosened knot, that lovely hair waving over her shoulders, opening the door with her finger at her lips, the almost-smile. . . . An anticipatory tingle ran over his lower abdomen and he felt the prickle of hair against his undershorts.

"I think I know the house," Doris remarked. "Near the library? It's rather distinctive."

"Especially since they painted it lavender," Anita agreed.

"I couldn't live in a house that color," Doris said.

"I don't have to look at it when I'm inside, thank heaven," Anita said. Doris looked confused, as if Anita, in her innocence, had just executed a smart flanking maneuver. She shot a glance at her husband.

He started doing sums in his head, that old schoolboy trick to keep his body from betraying what was in his mind, and sliced into a sausage with the edge of his fork. It sprayed a little stream of fat toward Anita. He felt his face go pale. Was everything to betray him?

But Doris hadn't noticed. She was eating her own eggs.

"I've got those exercises you assigned to do, still," Anita said. "If you'll excuse me, I'd better get at them."

"Exercises?" Doris asked.

"For the class," he explained.

"Exercises don't inspire me much, I'm afraid," Anita said. "I'll have to spend lunchtime sitting on my bench, and hope those thunderstorms they forecast blow over."

"What bench is that?"

"Down the trail to the lake." So she did use the bench. "I like to sit there with the trees, and the quiet. And my rhyming dictionary, I have to admit."

"You don't rhyme ordinarily?" Doris asked.

"Not ordinarily."

The glance from Doris seemed almost mocking. Surely not? "Doris," Davis-Williams said, done with the sausage and spreading jam on his toast. "She's got work to do." And thank God, he added mentally, or in a moment I'd have flung myself across the table and seized her on the spot! He toyed with the image of the table tilting, dishes and cutlery and bits of toast flying, Doris screeching the factory-whistle screech she usually reserved for centipedes in the bath, the consternation of the other breakfasters, until he decided that was too dangerous and buried his nose in his coffee cup.

Anita excused herself. He watched her pay her check—just toast and coffee—and go out onto the terrace, still shaded from the morning sun for half its length. She turned her head, nodded, and sat down with one of the older poets at a table near the south wing of the lodge. Alas, not a single glimpse of her firm white calves, of the blue hollows of her ankles!

Suddenly conscious of a voice beside him, he hauled his mind back.

"Headache," Doris was saying, index finger and

thumb pressed to her forehead above her eyebrows. "I'm seeing yellow flashes."

The air-conditioning failed, yet again, near the end of the morning class. Davis-Williams stared at the silent ventilator as if expecting it to launch a rocket attack. "We'll meet outside this afternoon, then, shall we?" he said dejectedly.

"What if it rains, like they're saying?" Little Aurora, whatever her name was, Dawn, that was it, with her anxious little face. She put her head down as he gazed at her, shy little thing like her verse—

He walked over to the west-facing window and peered out past a juniper growing just outside. A line of white clouds had appeared to the southwest, echoing the shapes of the trees that ringed the lake. They didn't look any more threatening than had similar clouds in the past few days; the rest of the sky retained its faded blue. "I don't think it will," he said. "But if it does, we can always move indoors."

"Let's hope it doesn't," McCready remarked. "The potters are having a picnic this afternoon."

"Oh, yes? Then, for all our sakes, we'll hope the rain holds off. But surely their picnic's tomorrow?"

"No, it's today," somebody said. "I saw the notice posted in the lobby. They're not supposed to eat in the dining room this noon."

"Such regimentation," Davis-Williams remarked. "Well, shall we get on with this?"

Half his mind had been busy all morning with a scheme to surprise Anita on her bench while Doris swam as planned with the Ammans family, but it was not to be: the headache had arrived and, terrified as always by his wife's pain, he agreed to take her place. He left Doris sitting by the open window of their room and went down to indulge himself with a double cheeseburger with bacon, lettuce, and tomato and a double-thick milkshake, since Doris wasn't there to tot up his cholesterol intake. He viewed this binge as just compensation for his tolerating those aggressively friendly *folks* in her stead.

After lunch he tiptoed into the room, where Doris was resting on the bed with a blanket half over her, to fetch his swimming suit.

"Aren't you hot, Dee?" he asked, with genuine concern. He could see that her face was beaded with sweat, even in the dimness of the room now that she had drawn the curtains.

"No." Even her voice was dim. "You know these headaches. I'm always cold. Just let me sleep, will you?"

He took the swimsuit with him, to change in one of the cabanas near the pool, and found himself still on tiptoe as he descended the stairs.

"Roz." Anita paused with her notebook clasped in both hands, her mouth grim. Roz felt her neck hairs rise. "Marybeth Saarinen asked me to speak to you."

"Yeah, huh?" Roz smoothed her hair up off her neck and pretended to study the effect in the mirror. "Heat's getting to her, is it?"

"I guess you could say that."

"Two lousy nights. She's not missing much, I'll tell you."

Anita's reflected face took on a pink gleam. "Roz, you really ought to leave those guys alone. I mean, it's their lives you're playing with. And for what?"

"They're big boys, lady," Roz blustered. As always when cornered, she went on the attack: "And who's talking? After screwing our Owen in the woods like an animal?"

Anita flushed. "I didn't, as you very well know."

"Yeah? You think that wife of his would believe that?"

Under Anita's steady gaze Roz tugged at the lower edge of her shorts. "We're staying out of each other's business, remember? I warned you what I'd do, remember? What if I trot back to Carlotta or Marybeth and say, wrong number, sucker, Anita's the one that's got your joker by the balls?"

Anita sat down on the end of her bed. "You crazy kid!" she exclaimed, louder than she'd spoken all week. "Can't you think of anything to do but make trouble? That's sick, Roz, that's really sick."

"Ah-ah!" Roz chortled, waving an index finger. "Scared you, didn't I? Well, let me tell you, just because you're old enough to be my mother doesn't mean you have to talk like her."

Anita's face didn't change at all; she kept that pale, steady, unnerving gaze fixed straight at Roz. *Maybe I will go to Carlotta, the bitch,* Roz thought. With a big grin and a shoulder wriggle that set her breasts bouncing, Roz opened the door and began to back out. Not even Anita could see through an act like this, she thought triumphantly.

"What would your father say?" Anita asked quietly.

Roz stiffened as the shot went home. She slammed the door behind her and clenched her eyes shut for a moment. The lodge. Distractions. With a sigh of relief, she pointed herself toward the terrace.

The clouds had come closer and grown darker, but still rain looked a long way off to an eye trained on a midwestern sky for the best part of an adult life. Davis-Williams estimated two hours, long enough to spend at least half the afternoon class outdoors. He came along the narrow hall that led from the pool into the lodge in time to see The Body burst from the dining room in high dudgeon, stop short, and put her hand to her lowered face. After a moment she turned and looked back into the dining room. More undercurrents. He shook his head sadly.

He continued on up to his room and softly opened the door, lifting so that the hinges wouldn't squeal, to see whether Doris felt any better. No: the room was still darkened, the curtains dead at the window despite the breeze outdoors. She was huddled under the blankets with the pillow over her head: it must be a bad one. Headaches. He gave the spill of hair across the blanket an exasperated glance, dropped towel and swimsuit onto the floor just inside the door and drew the door shut without a quarter of the violence he felt.

Down at the edge of the terrace half the class was already gathered, early as it was. Four or five yards away, among heads of clover bobbing in the southerly wind, a pair of mallards discussed the feasibility of approaching the humans for a handout in croaking undertones. The female examined the prospects with one eye and then the other and sidled up to Dorothy LaBruyere. Commendable accuracy. "Here you are, ducky," she said, pulling some bread from her tote bag and holding it out. The duck stopped to think it over, and the drake waddled up and snatched the bread.

"Men," said one of the older women.

"Do you think it'll rain?" Jack Saarinen asked.

Everyone but Dorothy, who was searching her bag for bread for the duck, looked at the sky. The line of clouds was darker and closer, but the sun still shone. "No," Davis-Williams said. "Worse luck. Except for the potters, of course."

A second pair of mallards, less shy than the first, dropped onto the lawn and made for the bread line.

The poets sat chatting in the lee of the lodge wing, dragged down by the humidity. The ducks found enough energy to squabble over the bread. Davis-Williams thought of his wife, upstairs under her blanket, and wondered if he should worry about heat stroke. His own shirt felt like a wet rag on his shoulders and ribs; the thought of blankets seemed almost obscene. In the end, his sloth won out and he promised himself to check on Doris if they should have to move, and sat still.

A bit past two-thirty he roused himself from his lethargy enough to glance at his watch. "Who's still missing?" he asked. "Perhaps we ought to begin." Begin what? He'd used up his stock of easy exercises the week before, and how was anyone to put two coherent thoughts in a row in this humidity?

"Roz and Anita." Dorothy LaBruyere was counting: he'd almost forgotten that he'd asked who was still to come. The cheeseburger was providing its own penance in his stomach; the tepid water of the pool seemed to be clinging to him still.

"And Moose, and Steve—or did he go on his wife's picnic?"

"No, he said he'd be here," someone supplied.

"And the Bobbsey Twi—Sue and Mim, I mean. . . ." She looked around. "Isn't that all?"

"We'll wait just a few minutes longer," Davis-Williams permitted himself. "Does anyone have any questions, in the meantime?"

Fourteen sweaty faces regarded him with less expression than a flock of sheep. He could understand if they couldn't formulate a single complete sentence among them; not just the heat, alas. This workshop had been nothing to look back on with pride.

"There's Roz," someone said.

The Body appeared at the edge of the woods. She stumbled onto the rough lawn in her ridiculous high sandals and ran toward the group, one arm waving and the other supporting her jouncing breasts.

"What's this?" Davis-Williams muttered. A small shock of alarm touched his wrists and throat.

"Probably she dragged some poor jerk into the woods and he didn't feel her up," one of the beards remarked lazily. "So she's coming to get a replacement."

Saarinen blushed.

"That's a real emergency," one of the older women said. The ducks scattered, squawking.

"No, something's very wrong," Davis-Williams realized, apprehensions coming in clouds. He untangled his legs and got to his feet. Roz stopped waving and grasped her breasts with both hands, running with short, jerky strides on the treacherous sandals. He could hear her gasp for breath: with the hair rising on his head he hurried to meet her.

"Anita," she gasped. "Come quick."

"Anita?" He noticed, with an odd sense of detachment, that he could no longer move. This, then, was what it meant to be rooted to the spot. How appropriate the old cliché proved! But then, most did.

"Dead," Roz choked. "Will you come on!"

One of the beards leaped to his feet and pounded across the lawn toward the gap in the pale aspen trunks where Roz had appeared. The roots dissolved and Davis-Williams found himself also running, easily catching up with the younger man. He could hear The Body running behind him, not stumbling anymore. A glance over his shoulder showed him why: she was carrying her sandals.

"Mind the bees," he called to her, and made for the wood with pumping fists and heart.

13

SHE HAD BEEN SITTING on the low bench that looked out over the lake: whoever or whatever had attacked her seemed to have pulled her backward across the halved log, so that her lower legs still rested across it. The light summer frock was thrown back across her hips, and what Davis-Williams first registered was not the dark blood that had soaked through from the wound in her chest, but the shadowed triangle showing through her silky panties. A confusion of nausea and desire claimed him. He could not turn away.

A jay went screeching through the trees over his head.

"Oh, dear God," he heard his own voice say. Without thinking, he reached for the skirt, to pull it up over her knees and restore her dignity, but the beard seized his wrist and stopped him.

"The police will want it left alone," he said.

"Oh, yes, the police," Davis-Williams gabbled. "Someone must call the police. I suppose I—"

"I'm not going back through these woods alone," Roz declared.

Slowly, the light was leached from the scene. "I— shouldn't someone stay with her?" How dark the gray eyes looked, staring through the canopy of leaves!

"You two stay here," said the beard. "I'll go."

"No, wait, I—" But the boy was already loping back the way they had come. Davis-Williams turned and warily faced The Body. Something of Anita, something alive, seemed still present. Perhaps only her scent. "I suppose she's really dead?" he asked.

"She's dead," Roz said dully. "I made myself feel for her pulse." She slumped down against a tree on the other side of the path and turned her head away. His heart was still beating as fast as it had when he'd first stopped running, and he laced his fingers over his ribs in a vague wish for more decorum. After a moment he felt in his breast pocket for the silver cigarette case he had carried there until two years before.

"God, I need a cigarette," Roz said.

The thought disgusted him although he'd had it himself not one second before. "The woods are too dry," he said. "We don't need a fire on top of this."

With the clouds now overhead the mosquitoes came out with a vengeance. He saw one on Anita's shin and wanted to slap it, reminded himself that it didn't matter. Tears welled in his eyes.

Roz got to her feet and began pacing up and down the path, going no farther than the bend toward the lodge and about the same distance in the other direction, kicking her heels against the bark chips even though she was still carrying the sandals. After several minutes it occurred to him that she might be destroying evidence.

"I don't think you should do that," he said.

"What?"

"Walk up and down like that."

"Well, Jesus, what do you want me to do? Kneel in front of her or something?"

He felt the rage bubble out of his belly and clenched his teeth against it. "No," he said, surprised at how calm he sounded. "It's just that he may have left clues."

"Oh, hell." Rozlynne looked down at her feet for a moment, her face anxious, and then continued pacing. "Too late now," she said at the end of her track. She made her turn and came back toward him. "Are you crying?" she asked.

The tears had run down his face with the sweat without his even becoming aware of them. Somewhere beneath the surface, his heart knew that Anita was dead, even while his mind still fought against the possibility. He looked at this from a distance, as if through a magnifying glass, while he unconsciously clutched the placket of his shirt.

The beard returned, accompanied by Stephen Mc-Cready. "The cops are on their way," he said. "Should be here soon."

"The class!" Davis-Williams remembered.

"I told them what happened, and they all went up to the Loft Bar, except Dorothy asked the shuttle driver to take her to the church in Coleridge. Only he wouldn't."

"He wouldn't?"

"It's called 'securing the perimeter,' " McCready said. "Who scuffed up the path like that?"

"That was me," Rozlynne said.

"You got no more sense than a rabbit, you know that, Roz?"

She turned her back, hugging her stomach, the sandals still dangling from her left hand. Davis-Williams remembered the rabbit, a red dangle from the Indian boy's hand, fancied that he'd heard the unlucky beast squeal as he entered the woods, what, only three days ago? Had Anita called out, cried for help, unheard?

For a moment, he thought he heard thunder.

"I'm going back to the lodge," Roz announced.

"I thought you'd never walk through the woods alone again?"

"Whoever it was is miles away by now, if he's got any sense," Roz said unsteadily. "Anybody got a cigarette?"

McCready supplied one, struck a light.

"Thanks." She drew on it hard, blew smoke. "See you."

Roz, still barefoot, walked quickly up the grassy slope toward the annex, not sure how much of a hurry she could afford to show. The stubby grass pricked at her feet, but she paid little attention. The cigarette was still in her hand; after a moment she glanced at it, surprised to see it there, and took another long drag as she examined the scene ahead of her. A solitary police car was pulling into the parking lot on the other side of the lodge. It drove down the sidewalk beside the pool and stopped, faced with a flight of steps to the lawn.

As she got closer to the annex the car disappeared from view behind the weathered cedar shingles of the wing of the lodge. Roz sighed and tossed the cigarette away onto the gravel path. Without bothering to put her shoes on, she took a few gingerly steps across the crushed stone and groped in her handbag for the key to the room. Had anyone noticed that she'd retrieved the bag from behind that tree? she wondered.

Nobody had been here since Anita left. Her own clothes, as usual, were strewn over bed and floor; she had long since abandoned the pretense of tidiness. Anita's half of the room maintained its customary good order. Roz crossed it as if it were haunted and took a facial tissue from the dispenser by the sink; with the tissue over her fingers she slipped Anita's black notebook out of her handbag and carried it into the bathroom. She locked the door.

Roz, whatever else she was, was not stupid. She turned the pages of Anita's journal by the edges, using only her long varnished nails, and while she gritted her teeth at Anita's superior tone where she herself appeared in the daily accounts, Roz destroyed nothing. She skimmed avidly until she reached the last page. No mention of the argument that noon, though she'd hashed out a couple of the others in the journal. . . . Roz sat quietly on the edge of the bathtub for several seconds. "Damn," she said softly. "She never slept with him, after all."

The click of the bathroom latch sounded loud to her ears, her own bare feet on the carpet might have been those of an elephant; the thunk of the journal into the drawer Anita kept it in was like the door of a dungeon slamming. Face contorted, Roz rammed the drawer shut. She sobbed once and brushed at her eyes with the backs of her hands, smearing brown eyeliner onto her temples. Half a minute later, somebody pounded at the outer door.

"Is Jack Peletier up at the lodge?" Sheriff Winton turned and looked back up the path.

"Yeah, I saw him by the desk."

"Get him down here. Maybe he can track something." As the deputy started for the lodge, the sheriff looked up at the gray sky, barely visible through the leaves over his head. "Call for the dogs, too," he yelled after the deputy. "See if we can get them here before it rains."

"Is it going to rain?" Davis-Williams asked.

"We're under a tornado watch," Winton replied. "Don't you keep the radio on in weather like this?"

The sheriff was wearing a light tan shirt and blue jeans, instead of the uniform Davis-Williams had expected. The man had the chubby complacency and the mild, contemplative smile of a toad, and Davis-Williams suspected that, like a toad, when an advantage came his way he would seize it so quickly that the flicker of his catch would never be seen: only, he thought with a shudder, the gulp as the man made the advantage his own forever.

"You can go on up to the lodge," Winton told him. "Just don't leave the grounds."

Davis-Williams nodded and struck across the cloud-dimmed grass for the lodge. Thunder rolled across the lake. Three police cars and an ambulance were parked in the end of the lot that showed beyond the south wing of the lodge. Could they be real? Could this be real? Wasn't it just something on the telly?

He crossed the dining room without speaking to anyone. The door at the end of the hall that led to the annex path clanked in a sudden wind; the man Moose strained against it to pull it closed. Davis-Williams flipped a hand and climbed the stairs, marveling that the lodge guests were all behaving as if nothing had happened. Perhaps, for them, nothing had happened: perhaps no one had yet spread the news; perhaps the biggest concern was still that the air-conditioning had wheezed to a halt once more. In the midst of life, he remembered. *In the midst of life we are in death.* The simple prayer book phrase conjured up an odor of damp and beeswax, chill, bewilderment.

Doris was lying in very nearly the same position as he'd left her in; she had thrown back the cover and shoved the pillow off her head and seemed now to be sleeping, the last stage of a headache. He tiptoed round the end of the bed and looked at her white, sweating face. He hadn't the heart to wake her. Instead, he decided to join the students in the bar. Lines of poetry beat in his head like tides, fragmented and rejoined into a rush of somber words that frightened him. Was this what Doris had felt, when the child had been stillborn?

Unfair, unfair. He was thinking only of a week's acquaintance, a dreamed-of dalliance . . . but what did Doris feel? What had Doris ever felt?

Unused to such questions, he hurriedly, silently, left the room and made for the bar. Light. Companions.

*   *   *

"Where's Anita?" Moose demanded.

"Moose, she's dead."

125

Moose grabbed the door frame with both hands, and a little noise came out of his mouth, like the sound of a man in mortal pain who has at all costs to hide. "I was hoping—I—did you really find her?"

Roz nodded.

"How? I heard somebody shot a deer the other day. Did she get shot by mistake?"

"Where did you get that idea?" Roz lifted her chin at him, and he noticed that her eye makeup had smeared, as it had after her outburst at the warming house. "She wasn't shot."

Moose felt his bowels turn cold. "Not shot?"

"Stabbed, I think, though I didn't check real close. Right up under her ribs, like this." Roz demonstrated an upward thrust.

"Oh, my God," Moose groaned. He hid his face against one forearm for a moment, then looked suspiciously at Roz. "How would you know?"

"I was a nurse's aide in the ER at Hennepin General last year. My father was in one of his debt to society moods, so I got the job." She shrugged. "Every other guy came in on a Friday night was stabbed. Moose, could you hold me?" she pleaded suddenly. "Just hold me, hold me, nothing else?"

The little noise happened again. "No," he said, and turned and tramped away up the gravel path. Roz looked after him until he disappeared among the spruce trees. A gust of wind barreled across the lawn and into the trees, setting them howling. She leaned the door shut and sank down on her haunches with her back against it, her face in her hands.

* * *

"You guys messed up the ground pretty good, eh?"

"Aw, there was a whole herd of jackasses here before us," the sheriff said. "Can you pick up anything off to the side, maybe?"

126

Peletier padded slowly up one side of the trail and down the other for several yards, careful to keep to the part that had already been disturbed. "Somebody buried something back there," he reported. "Before those few spits of rain we had Saturday night, though."

"Guess?"

"Rabbit guts, or squirrel? The yellow jackets been at it."

The sheriff nodded. "Anything else?"

"Somebody been sitting against that tree just across the way, this afternoon. Was she shot?"

"Blown over backwards?" Sheriff Winton jutted his jaw and sucked in his lower lip as he studied Anita's body from a couple of angles. "Could be, but it looks to me more like she was pulled off the bench from behind. Or maybe given a push. Skirt's over the wound, damn it. Where the hell's the doctor? He's sure taking his sweet time."

Peletier nodded. "That there could be a footprint, eh? See it?"

"No," the sheriff said, unembarrassed. He sighted along Peletier's pointing finger. "Oh, those broken leaves?"

"Yeah."

"Who knows? The ground's like rock, with all this heat and no rain to speak of. Why couldn't he've done it down by the lake, or along by the bog? Get me a picture of that, Tom," he said to a deputy with a camera. "Long lens."

"I know, I know."

The sheriff stuck his hands in his pockets and jangled his change.

"Get the dogs on that," Peletier suggested.

"I already sent for 'em." The sheriff looked up at what he could see of the sky. It was a darker gray than it had been, and had taken on a bluish cast, relieved by dim flashes of light. "If they get here in time. Looks like we're heading for a real gully washer."

"Sounds like it, too, eh?"

The two men stood listening to the silence of the woods: no birdsong, where moments before a flock of grackles had been quarreling. Even the gusty breeze had died: not enough wind to move an aspen leaf. Only the crunch of the path as one of the deputies shifted his weight, and the zing of the electronic flash recharging.

"Half an hour, that's all I want," Sheriff Winton said to the sky.

"You won't get it," Peletier said. A robin faltered into its evening song, wobbled through one repetition, and stopped.

"Hey, here comes the doctor. Maybe now we can get moving." The sheriff took his hands out of his pockets and strolled toward the men hurrying along the path from the lodge.

Davis-Williams stood at the western windows of the bar, a beer in his hand. The air-conditioning had given up, but he was shivering. Below him, not a sign of the activity under the crazy quilt of trees. Could it be real? he asked himself again. Could he actually have seen what he thought he saw, this afternoon? A band of rough water traveled across the lake and the trees started to toss as the wind hit them. A few large drops of rain rapped at the window, in which he could see some of his students reflected. Monday. Four-fifteen. Class ought to be in session. Class was not in session. So this must be real, mustn't it?

Beside him, Stephen McCready had thrust his hands so deeply into the pockets of his cut-offs that it seemed they should have appeared beneath the tattered lower edges. Rain suddenly strummed the window, as if the lodge had sailed into a wave that broke over its decks, and the roar of falling water began, the thrum of a sea that steadied, waveless.

"Damn sky sprung a hole," McCready said. "That lets out the dogs, I guess."

"Dogs?"

"Tracking hounds. I saw them going down from the parking lot, five minutes ago. More beer?"

"No, thanks." But McCready had already dived into the smokey, sweaty-smelling room, where no one was saying much and everyone was drinking more than usual. *Drunken old solipsists in a bar,* Davis-Williams thought, feeling obscurely that a fine old tradition was being upheld.

He accepted the cold bottle McCready thrust at him and turned back to the window, which rattled as the wind smashed into the lodge and thunder battered at the roof. The spruces down to his right whipped about in the wind. The lightning, he saw, was the tenderest shade of pink.

Fifteen or twenty minutes later a sheriff's deputy came dripping up to the bar to ask the names and addresses of all the students in the poetry class. "I'll take you one at a time," he said. "First, I want the dead woman's roommate."

"Not here," said several voices.

"In her room?"

"Don't bet on it," said one of the beards.

"Alphabetically, then, starting with who's here. Dawn Atkins? And after her, Miriam Dubbins."

Dawn, looking stringy-haired and subdued, got up to follow the deputy down the stairs. She stumbled on the top step and flashed it an angry glance. The rest of the students sat still for several seconds.

"I don't know anything," Miriam complained loudly. "Why should I have to go first?"

"You don't, Dawn does," Sue pointed out.

"Yes, but she doesn't know anything either, so she doesn't count."

Sue contemplated her friend, decided her logic had been helped along by the two frozen daiquiris she had drunk in such a hurry, and offered to buy her another.

Down in the woods, the dogs weren't having much luck.

This time, it was Bluetongue doing the questioning. His first question, oddly enough, was to inquire where Davis-Williams kept his heart.

"About here, I imagine," he replied, placing his right hand somewhat above his left nipple, as if pledging allegiance to the flag he'd never troubled to make his own.

"Right under the alligator," Bluetongue commented.

"Beg pardon?" A little indignant, he figured out the reference a moment later: an excusable delay, since he made a point of never wearing knit shirts.

Bluetongue had him recall all the events of the day, from the time he got up, through the discovery of Anita's body. Davis-Williams found the exercise tedious and unwelcome, stirring as it did the feelings he had had at each incident, feelings he now wanted to be rid of and to conceal. Feelings he *was* rid of: it struck him as he talked that he felt quite drained, quite empty. Dead.

"Who would have been her enemy?" Bluetongue asked.

Davis-Williams tried to think. "I can't say," he said at last. "She seemed very unassuming. Perhaps her roommate would have some idea, or—" He remembered the man Moose standing over her in the hall outside the dining room. Was that small scrap of conversation grounds for suspicion? He remembered the man standing back, hands in his pockets, and decided not. "One of the other students," he finished lamely.

"We'll be getting back to you," Bluetongue promised. If the promise had been meant to reassure, it failed. Davis-Williams went down the hall to wake his wife.

He found her seated at the dressing table, doing up her hair. "Bad news, Dee," he said.

"Oh?" She reached for a hairpin. "I'd have thought good. I see you're not drenched."

"Anita Soderstrom is dead."

"Good heavens!" Doris exclaimed. She thrust the pin into her chignon and followed it with another.

"Murdered, Dee." He took a breath that was close to a sob. "On the trail down to the lake."

"Some illegal hunter, I imagine." Her next few words were blotted out by a thunderclap. ". . . Fences down. Anybody might come through. Highly irresponsible."

"Doris, she's dead!"

She turned from the glass and looked directly at him for the first time. "Why, Owen, you're crying!"

He touched his cheeks and found them wet. "Because she's dead, Doris. You don't seem . . ."

"All right," Doris said impatiently. "She's dead. Regrettable, but I don't see why you should weep over her."

"Oh, Dee, don't you see? All that brightness lost. . . ."

"The world hasn't missed her so far," Doris said, standing up and shaking out her skirt. "I doubt it will miss her now. Dozens of other people you know have died, and you never wept over any of them."

Davis-Williams, at a loss for words, plumped down into the armchair and stared at his wife.

"I hope this rain cools things off," she said. "Is the dining room open? This headache has left me ravenous." With a little flurry of her skirts, the skirts she had always maintained were a symbol of femininity, she left the room. Symbols leave much wanting, her husband thought, and got up to follow her.

In the dark downstairs bar, Moose sat in a booth with an elbow on either side of a glass of amber liquid, his head clutched in his hands. "I do terrible things," he said to the girl opposite.

"What things?" She had shredded the cocktail napkin into bits not half an inch across, and now she began pleating the paper coaster.

"Like, one time I had this tear gas canister." He paused to scratch a mosquito bite. "And there was this loud party going on across the street, I couldn't sleep, you know? So I just took this thing and lobbed it over the fence like a grenade and ran like hell. Never thought till afterwards I could have just asked them to can it. Hell, I didn't know I did it, even, until afterwards."

The girl stared at him; she'd read about the incident in the newspaper. He'd been locked up for three days, she remembered. "Moose," she said. "What are you trying to tell me?"

"I don't know," he moaned. "I don't know."

14

A SERIES OF storms had passed during the night, leaving a few large damp patches on the flagging of the terrace, and one puddle in which fragments of chair seats and cedar siding glided by as Davis-Williams walked to the edge of the grass. A yellow plastic ribbon, glistening in the bright, clear air, had been stretched over each of the entrances to the network of paths through the woods. Nowhere left to go, then, and Doris had gone off with her new friend, the Ammans woman, for the day. How indignant they had been, that they needed permission from one of the sheriff's deputies to do so!

Once again, the police had shown more interest in Rozlynne Haddad than Davis-Williams could account for, even considering that she had shared a room with Anita. Rotten luck for The Body, he thought. He had called off the morning class, and now was searching for his students, to sound them out about the afternoon. Not that he felt he could concentrate on teaching, but when you got down to it, they'd paid for twenty-two class sessions, and they ought to get as many as possible.

No one was on the terrace but The Body—that is to say, none of his students. A few other guests chattered at the near-in tables, glancing at the yellow ribbons from time to time, but the weather had turned cool and the sun had yet to dry the chairs and tables; the terrace was unpleasant enough that ordinarily no one at all would have sat there. The Body looked rather forlorn, sitting by herself at one of the farther-out tables and squinting slightly at the sunlight on the lawn. He noticed that she had found some less revealing clothing than she usually wore, and then that the shirt she was wearing open over a low-cut blouse was not her own: it lacked two inches of being wide enough to button over her bosom. Since Doris was nowhere about, he yielded to sympathy and stopped at the table. "I hear you've had a bad time with the police," he said.

She jerked, and winced. "Some yo-yo in the next motel room told them I'd had an argument with Anita yesterday noon."

"Did you?" he blurted, astonished.

She nodded. "As a matter of fact. It wasn't the first, either, as my friend also told the cops." She flipped a hand at the seat opposite. "Sit down, if you want. Nobody else will."

"What on earth could you and Anita argue about?" He dumped a puddle out of a chair and perched on its edge.

"Oh, nothing, really." She pulled a cigarette out of a pack lying on the table and lit it, eyes screwed up against the smoke. "That's how come it was me that found her," she said. "I went looking for her to say I was sorry."

"Oh, my."

The Body half grinned at him, the corners of her mouth drawing down. "Oh, my, indeed," she said, with a faint return to her more familiar mocking tone. He didn't know what to say to that, so he said nothing. The brief twisting grin disappeared.

"They're saying I'm the one that should have died, not her," she said.

"Who's saying that?"

The Body jerked her head toward the lodge. "Them. All of them. Because, oh, they don't like the way I act."

"Nobody deserves to die," Davis-Williams declared.

"Oh, well, maybe extreme cases, like Adolf Hitler."

"Who?"

"Never mind." He blinked at the suddenness and enormity of the gulf between them. Buzz bombs, he thought, his ears straining at the memory.

"I didn't kill her," Roz said, bringing him back just as abruptly. "They're saying I killed her. That's ridiculous. I only knew her a week." She flicked the ash from the cigarette onto the paving, where it slowly sank into the damp. "Nobody gets that mad, in only a week."

"People often do lose their tempers," Davis-Williams pointed out.

"Uh-uh." The Body shook her head decisively. "Whoever did that had to go looking for her, just like I did. And she was easy to find, like I keep telling those cops. Everybody knew where she liked to sit, just like everybody knew where to find mostly everybody else. Over lunch, anyway."

Except me, he thought.

"You think she read somebody's journal?" Roz asked, her eyes narrowed. "Some of those exercises you had us do . . . no, Anita wouldn't have done that. She was straight."

He wished she would put out the cigarette. The victory over the poisonous weed two years before had been too hard won to give it up now, and he found himself greedily inhaling at every wisp of smoke that floated his way.

"Cigarette?" she offered.

"No thanks."

"I wish they'd let me go home. That's what I want to do, go home."

"That reminds me. I was looking for my students, to see if we should meet this afternoon."

The Body gave him an odd, blank look. "You can if you want," she said. "I don't think I'll come."

He nodded his head sideways. "As you like." I should get up and go now, he thought. Find the rest of them.

But he sat on, lacking even the energy to rise and say good-bye. The girl stirred.

"I did something kind of cruddy," she said. "Don't tell anyone, will you?"

"Of course not," he replied, not really interested.

"I told Carlotta McCready Anita was sleeping with Steve."

"Good heavens!" As he stared at her a little worm of curiosity ate its way out of its shocked cocoon. "Did she?"

Roz shrugged impatiently, the first time he had seen her shoulders move under cloth. "Of course not," she said. "Not Anita."

"But then, why . . .?"

"Too complicated to explain," Roz said. "Just something between Anita and me." She sighed, a long stream of smoke from both nostrils and mouth. "I just wish I hadn't." After a moment she reached out and ground the cigarette out in an ashtray so damp that the glowing coal hissed. "Forget I said anything," she added. "I'm sorry I did. So forget it."

"Okay."

"I'm going back to the room and see if the cops are done with it," she said, standing.

"Okay."

Left alone and lethargic at the table, Davis-Williams watched the girl pick her way through the damp clover blossoms toward the yellow doors of the annex. What was it like to be so young? For the life of him, he could not recall. And yet, only a few days before, he had felt the fizz of new love . . . of infatuation. Now he couldn't even imagine what sort of quarrel Roz might have had with Anita, to say such a thing about her. . . .

The yellow door closed behind Roz, long after he had failed to follow the thought to the end. After a few minutes he willed himself to stand, to turn toward the lodge, to walk past the few curious guests that stared at him, to enter the dining room. Deserted. He went on up to the lobby, borrowed pen and paper, and wrote out a notice to pin up on the bulletin board beside the desk, to say that the Poetry Workshop would meet in the downstairs lounge at two-thirty for those who wanted a class.

He pushed the thumbtack in with more vigor than it needed and stood back. Legible enough. But oh, he was tired, tired! What was the matter with him? He hardly had the strength to mount the stairs to wash up for lunch.

The door of the room stood open. Doris sat in the armchair checking some unfortunate scrap of vegetation against *Common Wildflowers of Minnesota.*

"Idiot plant," she said, as he entered the room. "It's got to be hoary alyssum, but the petals are blue. What do you make of that?"

"Not much," he said, dropping onto the edge of the bed. "I thought you weren't coming back until afternoon?"

"Oh, the paths are wet, and it's getting too steamy and buggy in the woods."

"I thought the paths were blocked?"

Doris grinned. "Not if you know where to go. Judy and I walked up the road a bit—that's where I picked this—" She frowned at the book in her lap. "Habitat's right. But those petals! A new variety, perhaps?"

He waited, but she continued to frown at the book. "You were saying?"

"Saying? Oh, yes. We went into the woods the back way. She's quite good on insects, Judy is, did you know? Not many people know insects. But it did get rather unpleasant, so we came back. She decided to lunch with Roger, and they're off somewhere."

"I was just thinking of lunch, myself." He stood up and went into the bathroom.

"Would you mind if I came?" Doris called. He was

already running water to wash his hands and wasn't sure he'd heard correctly. Annoyed, he shut the water off.

"What?"

"Would you mind if I came?"

"Of course not," he snapped, even more annoyed, and turned on the tap full force.

The class, ill attended and dreadfully disorganized, was the predictable disaster. Davis-Williams collected his wife and went up to the bar afterward, to find the remainder of his students sitting in small groups, drinking. "All emulating Dylan Thomas," Doris remarked. "I hope you don't intend to spend the evening?"

"Just one slow drink before dinner," Davis-Williams said. "I'd think, considering that one of my best students has just been murdered, that you'd understand?"

Doris smiled and ordered lemonade. Despite her smugness, she seemed nervous, playing with the rings on her left hand, tapping her blunt fingernails on the table, twisting about in the chair to look at the others. Davis-Williams discovered that the bar stocked an Irish whisky and buried his nose in its peaty aroma. No one came up to speak to him, an unaccustomed situation he couldn't fathom, despite the covert examination he made of the room. The Body was quite right, he observed. She sat at a table near the windows, conspicuously alone and more wan than wanton, gazing into a snifter of some milky-looking concoction. At rest—no wriggles, no lip-licking, no arching of brows—she looked scarcely old enough to be served without question.

His whisky slowly paled in the glass. Impossible to get it without ice, apparently; the middle-aged bartender seemed in a state of shock deeper than his own. At last he settled for draining the liquid off the cubes. "Let's go," Doris said instantly.

"I thought I might have another."

138

"Have it in the dining room, while we wait to be served."

"All right," he sighed, too weary to insist. She rose and picked up her handbag and fussily pushed a pin more firmly into her hair. Across the room, Rozlynne Haddad had come to the end of her piña colada and was heading for the stairs. They met at the end of the railing that encircled the stairwell: Davis-Williams was appalled to see how waxen she was, how blank her gaze. Who would have thought he would ever miss that suggestive sparkle?

Doris held back to let Roz go first, but he remembered his manners in time to precede the women down the stairs. His heel caught in a loose bit of carpet at the top. "Say," he said, half turning. "There's a loose—"

Too late. With a small peep like a frightened sparrow, Roz tumbled into him. He staggered against the handrail, put an arm out to catch her. The force of her fall against his arm spun him into the wall. His head made a dry sound like a thumped coconut against the pine paneling. He felt her slip past his hand, heard a small rip as some part of her clothing caught on his watchband, and then he was stumbling down the steps to save himself while Roz fell headlong into a moaning sprawl on the floor below.

Doris thudded past as he clutched at the railing for balance. "Don't touch her!" she cried. "Don't move her!" In a moment she was kneeling over Roz, asking where it hurt and raising her voice to demand an ambulance, a doctor.

"I'm a doctor," said the fat-kneed man who stooped beside her.

Davis-Williams sat on the bottom step in a daze. Legs appeared and disappeared before him. Someone stopped and leaned a face into his to ask if he were all right. He nodded. Far away, a siren sounded.

He huddled against the stairwell wall as the yawping

ambulance drew nearer, colder even than the recovered air-conditioning could claim credit for. For several minutes, the legs around him wore white trousers. Then there were no more legs, and the spot where Roz had lain was empty.

"Come along, Owen," Doris demanded. "We've yet to have dinner."

Would nothing destroy the woman's appetite? "I'm not hungry," he said.

"Stand up, do. People will think you're drunk. A full professor!"

He stood up and let her lead him downstairs to the dining room and accepted the glass of whisky she ordered for him. Slowly it warmed his gut, slowly his eyes focused on the menu. "I'm not hungry," he repeated.

"You've only eaten one meal the whole day," Doris said. "And not much of that."

He shook his head and closed the menu. "Not hungry."

"I am."

He sat and watched her eat.

Doris chattered her way through batter-fried broccoli, salad, a succulent steak charred without and rosy within, potato, cheese and biscuit, and a large dish of Haägen-Dazs ice cream. She was just spooning up the last of the latter when Sheriff Winton drew out one of the two empty chairs at their table and sat down.

"Pretty bad workshop, hey, Professor Williams?" he asked.

"Davis-Williams," Doris corrected. The man ignored her, instead watching her husband nod. What is Owen looking so sheepish about? Doris wondered.

"First one of your students gets herself killed," the sheriff observed. "Now another one falls down the stairs."

Davis-Williams drew a deep breath. "It does seem uncommonly unlucky," he admitted.

The sheriff watched him closely, his round, wide-mouthed face in repose. "She says you pushed her," he said.

"What?"

"Haddad. Says you pushed her down the stairs."

"No, not at all!" Davis-Williams protested. "Quite the opposite! I was ahead of her on the stairs, and I caught my heel in a bit of loose carpet, and I turned round to tell her—and my wife, of course—to be careful, and just then she also caught her heel and fell. I tried to catch her," he added, looking into the tail end of his fourth whisky, "but she fell so heavily, I couldn't. I almost fell, myself."

"That's absurd," Doris was saying, all the while he maneuvered his tongue around this speech. "Owen wasn't in any position to push the child. And why should he?"

"There's a rumor," the sheriff said, taking a cup of coffee from the waitress with a wink, "that you were in love with Anita Soderstrom."

"What! But I barely knew her!" The blood drained from his face. "And she's dead. *Nil nisi bonum,* and all that, but she was a very ordinary woman, apart from her poems. A little sickly looking." Doris narrowed her eyes and tilted her head to the left. "Just one of my students, that's quite all." The sheriff said nothing, his head cocked at attention. "A particularly good writer, nothing more," Davis-Williams blurted into the man's silence. "I had great admiration for her work. Have. But to say I was in love with her, a woman I had known only a week!" Doris's head jerked left. He caught the signal, finally, and subsided.

"And that you thought Miss Haddad had murdered her." The sheriff drew the whisky glass away from

Davis-Williams and substituted the black coffee. "And you wanted to get even."

"Not I," he insisted, breathless.

"There are other rumors," the sheriff said. "Such as that Soderstrom turned down your advances, and you killed her in a rage. . . ."

"Nonsense," Doris said. "I've enraged him regularly for twenty-seven years, and he hasn't killed me yet."

"Doris," he protested. "You know that's not true. And I wasn't anywhere near her," he said to the sheriff. "I didn't even see her, from the time she left class in the morning until The Bod—Miss Haddad came running—"

"Mmmm?" Winton prompted, when he stopped.

"And I'm a terrible shot, and I haven't a gun," he concluded.

"What's a gun got to do with it?"

"I'd heard she was shot?"

"No." The sheriff appeared to consider his words carefully. "Actually, she was stabbed with a serrated knife. Maybe even this one," he said, picking up the steak knife that hadn't been cleared from Doris's place. She made a gesture of horror.

"Sheriff Winton, I must protest," Davis-Williams said unevenly. "My wife has just eaten dinner."

"Not likely this knife," the man conceded, replacing it on the table. "Every second restaurant in the county has knives like this one."

"If Miss Haddad says I pushed her, then you must have talked to her?" Davis-Williams belatedly deduced.

Sheriff Winton nodded.

"Then, may I ask, is she all right? No bones broken?"

"Two badly sprained ankles and a back injury. There's some question how bad the back is. She might not walk again."

"Oh, dear." The words were hushed: he stared at the blue tablecloth in a state of semi-paralysis himself, trying to imagine that girl who had flaunted her beautiful legs with such abandon being wheeled about in a chair.

"Incidently," the sheriff said, "Miss Haddad asked me to tell you, Mrs. Williams, that she's grateful for your help after she fell."

"Davis-Williams," he murmured.

Doris nodded graciously. "All anyone would do," she said.

"Keep yourself available, Williams," the sheriff said, standing up.

"I've four more weeks to teach, after this one," he said, regarding the prospect with dismay. He found himself sipping the coffee, black as it was, and put the cup down with a shudder.

How Doris could expect him to bed her, after the past two days and the best part of a bottle of whisky, was beyond his feeble comprehension. He gave it a try, only to prove what the porter in *Macbeth* has to say about desire provoked by liquor, and then proved him also correct in remarking that it kills the performance.

Doris got up and slept in the other bed.

15

FRIDAY MORNING. FIVE days, and the yellow plastic ribbons were still stretched across the entrances to the lake trail. The balloons of their spirits, which might ordinarily have soared when the sheriff and his deputies departed, remained tethered by those ribbons as surely as if the yellow plastic had been bound around their hearts; the class had, by common consent, met in the lounge all the rest of the week, even though the air-conditioning had failed twice and the hot weather had returned. Davis-Williams strove to give his best to his teaching, partly to make up for his desultory performance of the week before, and partly as a kind of memorial—he knew the idea to be absurd, but he couldn't shake it—to Anita Soderstrom.

Doris had called the local hospital a couple of days before, to find that Rozlynne Haddad had been transferred to the Hennepin County Medical Center, in Minneapolis, to be closer to her parents' home.

"Can you imagine, a young girl like that living on her own, and her parents not ten miles away!" she had reported. "And behaving the way she did!"

"Perhaps she behaves differently with her parents nearby," he had suggested; Doris only sniffed, and he went back to reading his book.

At noon on that Friday, he finished dissecting the sonnet form in three of its variations, standing with his back to the cold fireplace and clasping his hands behind him. "We'll choose this afternoon what we're to read tonight," he announced.

"Oh, are we still reading?" someone asked.

"I think so, yes. It's on the agenda for every class. Do you think we should cancel?"

"Under the circumstances . . ." grandmotherly Dorothy LaBruyere said. She stopped. "But I saw it posted in the lobby."

"Oh, yes? Then perhaps . . ."

They discussed the reading in another dozen unfinished sentences and agreed to come to a decision that afternoon. "In any case," Davis-Williams promised, "I'll give you some tips on reading poetry for an audience, should any of you ever want to do so."

The group shuffled out of the room, not even murmuring to one another, although Davis-Williams knew that the murder of Anita and The Body's close call were passionately discussed in his absence.

"I thought you'd never finish," Doris said, taking his elbow in her hand as he emerged from the room. "Rog and Judy are waiting for us."

"Waiting?"

"Lunch, Owen. What's the matter with you? We arranged all this last night, remember? They're leaving this afternoon."

They. Ammans. "Oh, yes."

He couldn't work up much enthusiasm: Judith Ammans was all right, he supposed, and she did take up much of Doris's energy, leaving him free of it. Roger's manner was far too hearty for Davis-Williams's taste, and the children, while not ill-behaved as children go, were just short of unbearable simply by dint of being children. One lunch? Surely possible, surely he could put on a sociable face for Doris's sake for, what? An hour?

The Ammans family had already secured a table for

six, and Doris waved back at them with both hands, plowing toward them like the *Queen Elizabeth* at full cruising speed. He followed, very consciously in her wake, and made the right noises as he came up to the table and took the last chair, the one around which every waitress would have to step on her way out of the kitchen.

"You haven't heard any more from the sheriff, have you?" Roger Ammans inquired.

"No."

"Dreadful, that they can let such people run about loose," said Judith. The sheriff, does she mean? Davis-Williams wondered, while noting with amusement that his wife's British accent had rubbed off on Judith's South Dakota twang in the past two weeks. "A resort like this," she continued. "They certainly charge enough; you'd think they could keep the riffraff out."

Probably not the sheriff.

"Owen tells me he saw a boy kill a rabbit in the very spot that girl died, can you imagine?" Doris remarked.

"Only that he had one with him, Dee," he objected. Put as she had said it, too much significance seemed attached.

"There's a big difference between killing a rabbit and killing a woman," Ammans said, for once echoing Davis-Williams's own thought. "For one thing, you can eat the rabbit."

Doris looked slightly ill, but her husband had no sympathy for her; it was she who had mentioned the rabbit. Mercifully, rabbit was not on the menu, only walleye pike: Davis-Williams ordered the Spanish omelet.

Somehow, they got through lunch. Or, to be more precise, somehow, Davis-Williams got through lunch: the other three adults were quite happy to eat together and gossip about the two weeks just past, and the children were engaged in a sort of under-the-table warfare

146

that kept them nicely occupied. They parted with an exchange of addresses and promises on the part of the women to write often; Davis-Williams, thinking of that evening's planned reading, came back to the conversation just in time to realize that Doris had just bartered away some of his Guggenheim time to go and visit the Ammans's home in, which Dakota was it? He was about to object when his name was paged from the lobby.

"Excuse me," he muttered, and went gladly up the stairs to see Martin Jonas.

"You're having your reading, I see," Martin greeted him. "How about bringing your poets to our kiln opening afterwards?"

"Oh, are you done firing?"

"Sure, it's been cooling since last night. Porcelain. Should be some good stuff in there," Martin said, rubbing his hands together. "Oh, exciting! And no burned fingers. It'll be stone cold by then."

The phrase gave Davis-Williams goose bumps. "Fine," he managed to say. "I'm sure my people will want to come."

"Champagne all round," Martin said.

"Champagne?" Dismayed, he wondered what to say. "Er, perhaps a still wine, Martin? We poets aren't feeling very, uh, celebratory."

"Oh, point." Martin rocked on his toes and heels, his mouth drawn into a tight little pucker. "Yes, point. A nice white. I'll send Peletier into Coleridge to get a couple of jugs, right away, and I can have them cooling."

"You knew her, didn't you?" Davis-Williams asked.

Martin gave him a panicky glance. "Who?"

"My student. Anita Soderstrom. The one who, ah, died."

"No, no," Martin said, backing away. "What gave you that idea?" He hurried toward the desk, muttering something about Coleridge, and Peletier. Davis-Williams looked after him with his mouth slightly open. He shut it with a snap and looked for Doris, thinking of how the chairs should be arranged for the reading . . . if there was to be a reading. He remembered quite suddenly that it hadn't been decided.

Yes. They would read. His students spent the better part of the afternoon reading snatches of their poems and asking one another's advice; Davis-Williams developed a dull ache just below the margin of his ribs, thinking of how Anita Soderstrom would have shone in such a setting. In any setting. The ache didn't worry him: pent tears, that was all, he assured himself.

Doris helped to arrange the chairs after a quick supper. The poets began to straggle in nearer seven-thirty. A few minutes later some potters and some miscellaneous strangers showed up, and then Martin, who stood tugging at his mustache and watching the chairs fill, and helped to unfold some more when the seating ran out.

"Quite a crowd," he remarked. "I don't remember seeing such a turnout for one of your readings before."

Davis-Williams sighed. "It's not poetry bringing them, it's the smell of blood," he said bitterly. The people edging into the room now were ordinary resort guests, bright in pastel shorts and shirts, people who had seen the announcement in the lobby and hoped to pick over some juicy details, the sort Doris called "double-knit people." Davis-Williams set his jaw, remembering other readings, other years, when he had been as excited as Martin seemed to be about the kiln opening, when he had wanted to dragoon these people to come and hear his students read. "I'm afraid they're going to be disappointed," he added. "We've agreed to read only light poems."

His students were by this time sitting in a semicircle facing the audience, nervously fingering their pieces of paper. Three poems each, from the fourteen left—four had gone home at midweek, as soon as the sheriff had let them—should take about an hour. At quarter to eight he strolled to the center of the semicircle, to say a few words of introduction. They'd sat roughly in alphabetical order, for no reason he knew of, and it was Dawn Atkins who rose first, her poems trembling in her hands, to read about gooshy clay and porcelain, "white with fire."

The potters applauded politely, and so did most of the other guests. Mim Dubbins stood up as Dawn sat down, and droned on about clover and bees.

Davis-Williams stifled his yawns. Halfway through the reading he declared a brief intermission, which opportunity the lodge guests took to reduce the audience by half. The students read faster and faster, their heads dipped to their pages; the poems took on a nursery-rhyme rhythm. At last, the last student sat down. The potters produced another spattering of polite applause.

"Shall we adjourn to the ceramics studio?" Davis-Williams called out. The poets got up and stretched and began to talk to one another; the potters stampeded for the door.

"I think I'll skip the kiln opening, if it's all the same to you, Martin," Doris said. "I seem to be getting another headache, and the crowd and the wine will only make it worse."

"Oh, of course," Martin said. "You can see the pots in the morning, if you want. I'll ask Greg about that weed jar you saw him throw, if you're still interested. We fired stoneware Tuesday, and it came out pretty well."

"Thanks." Doris put on a brave smile. She shook Martin's hand and took herself off.

"Pity about her headaches," Martin said.

"Oh, I don't know. They keep her from dropping to skin and bone—she has the appetite of a young tiger when they go," Davis-Williams said.

"Well, let's get up the hill and get the bricks out of the way." Martin rubbed his hands together. "I always think unloading the porcelain firing is the best part of the session, don't you?"

Davis-Williams, who didn't care one way or the other about pots, smiled sadly. He recognized Martin's enthusiasm as something that should have been his, that had been his in other years, and that he missed bitterly. Once again, he and his students straggled up the path to the warming house. At the kiln shed, although the light was still not gone, Martin switched on the floodlights strung on long orange extension cords from the studio, and two of his students began removing the firebricks that had closed the kiln for the firing, stacking them carefully to one side. "Can you see anything yet?" potters kept asking.

"Oh, yes," said one of the brick-stackers. "That celadon bottle of yours looks good on this side. . . ."

Davis-Williams wrinkled his nose against the faint sulphurous odor exhaled by the still slightly warm kiln. It seemed to take forever for the door to come down, and the two students to start handing out the pots on the top shelf. Some of the nervousness of the potters transmitted itself to him; he shifted uneasily as the pots were passed through the crowd to their makers.

"Damn," said a voice. "It's got a red stain on the side. Who's the jerk who used the copper?"

"Carelessness," Martin muttered beside him.

"Here's your blue crystal," said a second voice. "Oh, it's flashed, too!" The tension among the potters increased; Davis-Williams noticed that the heat had made them all sweaty. He heard dirt scuffled under a shoe as one of the poets quietly left the group and returned down the path. A screw cap rang against a bottle: the remaining poets had apparently started on the wine. Davis-Williams pressed his lips against another yawn as he accepted a plastic cup half-full of pale yellow fluid. He stood sipping it as the first rank of shelves came down.

"Now what?"

Martin left his side and moved forward as someone called, "Come look at this, Martin. This jar's got a funny bulge on the side. I never saw anything like that before, did you?"

Martin took the jar and tugged at the elegant knob of the lid. "Looks like something inside deformed it," he said. "Lid's stuck. Get me a hammer, somebody."

"Whose is it?" someone asked.

"Mine." Such disappointment, compressed into a single syllable! Davis-Williams thought. What is it like to entrust the best your hand and brain can do to the vagaries of fire? He thought of his own annoyance at the occasional typo in a poem as Carlotta McCready held out her hands for the jar and tugged at the lid to no avail. "But there wasn't anything in it, just glaze," she said.

A hammer was handed through the crowd and Martin reclaimed the jar. He squatted to set it on the ground in the light of the floodlights and began gently tapping the edges of the lid with the wooden handle of the hammer. After a moment there came a musical *ping!*

"That's got it." Martin sat back on his heels and lifted the lid of the jar, glanced into it, and clapped the lid back on and turned to Davis-Williams.

"Owen." His Adam's apple jerked twice. "I think you'd better go call the sheriff."

The jar sat on one of the dusty tables in the studio. Of the potters, only Martin and Carlotta McCready remained. Davis-Williams had stayed on, too, partly out of a vague feeling of responsibility and partly out of a formless dread.

Sheriff Winton and Martin had their heads together over the mouth of the jar. "You see," Martin said, in his most pedantic voice, "that reddish discoloration could be from the copper rivets that held the handle on. Copper's notorious for migrating through the kiln atmosphere. You can see that it melted, and I bet some combined with salts in the glaze and traveled as a vapor. We had some red flashing on other pieces near it."

"Flashing?"

"Stains. That other roughness, the greenish stuff, is from the wood ash, when the handle burned, and—"

"Yeah, sure," the sheriff interrupted. "I can see all that. The big question is, how did it get there?"

Martin shrugged.

The sheriff regarded him for a moment. "Who put it in there to get baked?"

"Fired," Martin corrected. "Carlotta?"

"I wasn't here. Last I knew, I did the glaze and put it on the shelf."

"When was that?"

"Sunday? No, Monday morning. Yes, because then we all went on the picnic and nearly got drowned."

"And it's been sitting there ever since?" Winton asked.

"Until Wednesday evening, when we stacked the kiln," Martin replied.

"Who would have had a chance to put a knife in it?"

Martin replaced the lid on the jar very deliberately, turning it until the shapes of lid and jar matched and the lid sat without rocking. "Any potter," he said. "Anybody passing by when nobody was in the studio, or even just when this end of the studio wasn't in use."

"No," Carlotta said. "The spring on the screen door makes too much noise for that."

Martin looked up at her. "Oh, point," he said.

"Don't you lock up?" Winton asked. He turned to look at the shrouded moose head over the bar.

Martin followed his gaze. "Not without any liquor in

here. Pots are no good to anybody till they're done, and then the kids take them away."

"What about those lumps of clay?"

"Oh, point."

"What's a point?" Davis-Williams asked, impatient with the increasing obscurity of the conversation.

"The guy that put the knife in the pot held it down with a couple of lumps of clay," Martin said. "I guess so it wouldn't rattle."

"What good would that do?"

"Keep anybody from finding it before the jar was fired, I guess." Sheriff Winton's eyes narrowed ever so slightly. Danger, Martin, Davis-Williams thought. Here comes the flash of the toad-tongue, watch out. "Worked, but it was a slim chance," Martin continued. "If Carlotta had loaded her own work, she'd have felt the extra weight the instant she picked the thing up."

Carlotta nodded.

"Whoever did load it probably just thought it was a little heavy for its size," Martin went on. "Porcelain's hard to throw, lots of potters get it kind of thick the first few times. No reason to look inside."

"You realize what this means, don't you?" the sheriff asked. "The murderer is almost certain to be one of the people in your class. Who else would have the knowledge?"

Davis-Williams shut his eyes against the bald fluorescent light and groaned. "Every one of the poets. We toured the studio last week, and even I remember somebody telling us that jars are fired with their lids in place."

"That so?" Winton wrinkled his forehead at Martin.

"And we have odd people dropping by all the time," Martin added. "People find out there's a ceramics class, and they come up from the lodge to watch us work, ask a lot of dumb questions. Nuisance, really."

Davis-Williams reached for the jar. "May I look?"

"Sure."

He held it up to the light. The serrated blade of the knife was a shape he'd seen daily: it had come from the lodge dining room. The steel was now gray and somewhat bent. The part that had been covered by the wooden handle was now naked, and the two holes for the copper rivets stared emptily. The glaze inside the jar was pitted and uneven, muddy-colored, and the copper, covered with a greenish haze, was mixed with it.

"An awful shame," he said, holding the jar at arm's length. "It would have been a lovely piece."

Carlotta nodded. She felt her mouth draw down, tried to pull it up in a smile and failed. Tears gathered in her eyes and she rubbed them angrily. "What a rotten two weeks," she protested. "First that slut knocks half my pots off the shelf and breaks them, and now this, my best piece of porcelain ruined! Why my work? Why me?" She bounced out of the chair and ran to her purse for a tissue. As she stood over the open handbag, a sob broke from her gut; she fought tears again and lost.

"What slut is that?" Winton called to her.

"Rozlynne Haddad," she choked. She put her nose and forehead against the steel upright of the shelves her purse rested against and let herself sag.

"Tell me about Rozlynne Haddad," the sheriff said.

He had his toadlike look again, Davis-Williams saw with a stirring of terror. The tongue was about to flicker once more—first Martin, now Carlotta. Who knew what they would be digested into?

"Ah, she raised a ruckus the other day," Martin said as Carlotta returned to her seat.

"No, *I* raised the ruckus," Carlotta said firmly. "She was messing around with my husband. It wasn't the first time, and I told her to quit." She turned the jar so that she could look at its least blemished side. "It was the day I made this," she commented. Her mouth tucked into a wry grin. "It was on the wheel when she came in."

"Oh, really?" Sheriff Winton sat back in his chair. "Would you like to tell me where you were on Tuesday evening?" he asked. "Just before dinner, say?"

"Me?"

"You."

"Up in the Loft Bar." Something of Davis-Williams's uneasiness must have touched her, because she gave the poet the merest shadow of a glance before fixing the sheriff with a stare. "Why?"

16

OWEN DAVIS-WILLIAMS WAS a poet, not a policeman, so it had never entered his head that clues could fizzle.

After the kiln opening, he wasn't surprised that the deputies were back, to question the remaining poets before they left on Saturday. He found it no hardship to give them the Saturday morning. But he was astounded when all the poets scattered to their homes, the deputies left, and no one seemed to know anything more, beyond the bare fact that the knife with which Anita Soderstrom had probably been killed had been found.

Davis-Williams's acquaintance with police procedure was limited to following Roderick Alleyn through his adventures, and then only when he was in one of those long fallow stretches that sometimes comes upon a writer. Dame Ngaio Marsh had never once left her hero with insufficient clues, or even saddled him with any extraneous ones, so far as Davis-Williams could recall. A major rearrangement of his own mental furniture was required, simply to understand that merely knowing where the knife had been discarded was not enough, that the fingerprints that show up in detective novels on every other page are helpful in so few real-life situations that it is a tribute to the tenacity and thoroughness of real detectives that they bother about them at all—and that, in this case, whatever fingerprints might have existed on the knife had been burned away in the first stages of the firing of the kiln. He had no idea that the yellow ribbons he so deplored had been placed to keep people out of the way while the woods were searched square foot by square foot in hope of finding that knife, no idea that the mud of the lake bottom had been explored for fifteen yards out, no idea that the shuttle into Coleridge had suddenly become unreliable because Jack Peletier had used his keen eyes and long experience to try to pinpoint a place from which someone might have thrown a weapon into the bog, or that on Friday morning metal detectors held over the muck had located a dozen or more metal objects, each of which had been dug up: a trap with the bones of a woodchuck still in its jaws, a folding cup, the rusted head of a hatchet.

With the poets gone, he and Doris were rather at loose ends. Because the Fourth of July holiday shortened the next week, the second workshop began a full week after the first ended. Doris did some energetic tramping over the many hiking trails of Seven Slopes, and he dutifully trailed after her with his pockets filling with interesting sprigs of assorted weeds.

On the Fourth, they drove to the county seat to see a fireworks display and stayed overnight. On impulse, he stopped at the courthouse the next morning to see what Sheriff Winton had discovered since he'd seen the man last, half expecting to be told that one of his students was even at that moment on his way up from the Twin Cities in handcuffs. From the Twin Cities, because although others had come from every part of the state and even adjoining ones, Davis-Williams couldn't help but think that The Body was right: nobody gets that mad in a week.

Sheriff Winton, to his surprise, was in his office and willing to see him.

"You want to know what's happening with the Soderstrom and Haddad cases," the man said, grinning widely.

"Yes. Particularly the, ah, Soderstrom case."

"Nothing."

"Nothing!" Davis-Williams stared at the sheriff. Here he was, an elected official sitting in a reasonably pleasant office furnished with the taxpayers' money—and while Davis-Williams wasn't a citizen and couldn't vote, he most certainly paid taxes—which furnishing included a bank of gray, efficient-looking file cabinets, a swivel chair that didn't even squeak, a desk with a sufficiently large surface to work on—and the man could blandly say *nothing!*

"I suppose you don't have many murders in northern Minnesota," he ventured.

"Not many, no," the sheriff agreed. "And usually something simple, like a guy taking a shotgun to his wife after thirty years of nagging."

"When do you expect to make an arrest?"

"Maybe never."

Davis-Williams shook his head violently. "I've been teaching up here for years and years," he said, "and never before—well, I don't have to tell you it's always been peaceful, nothing remotely like this. But I can't accept that you'd let someone get away with murder!"

"Mr. Williams, let me tell you something." Winton leaned forward in his silent chair and tapped his index finger on the polished surface of his desk. "Life isn't often tidy. Crime is never tidy. The hardest crime in the world to solve is when a stranger up and kills another stranger."

"You just told me you didn't have much experience with murder," Davis-Williams protested. He felt himself flush and carefully picked his way past his anger. "Why don't you get somebody in who knows what he's doing?"

Winton leaned back in his chair. "I appreciate your opinion, Mr. Williams," he said, showing his political side. "I assure you, we know what we're doing. We have the resources of the entire state behind us. But, as I say, when you have this sort of crime, it becomes extremely difficult to bring the guilty party to justice. It's hard here, and it's hard in New York City, where they have damn near as many murders in a month as we do in the whole state of Minnesota in a year—so practice doesn't make perfect."

Davis-Williams snorted in frustration.

"I know, I know. A good-looking, talented, intelligent woman like that, you want to get to the bottom of it. Believe me, I'm trying. I had an investigator down in Minneapolis just Monday, talking to Cary Ellis—that's her apartment mate—to see if any of these people up here could be friends or acquaintances from before. We went through the entire guest list of the lodge for the whole nine days. And nothing."

"I see," Davis-Williams said, chastened.

"We learn patience in this job, Mr. Williams. You can't crack a new-laid egg and get a chicken, you know. You've got to set a hen on it and wait for it to hatch."

"Quite."

"Oh, and the Haddad business."

"Do you think she'll recover?" Davis-Williams asked mechanically, still thinking of Anita.

"Not yet." The sheriff looked at him expectantly. Davis-Williams stared back, wondering what it was the man expected. "I thought you'd want to know if she still claims that you pushed her?"

"Oh, that. I suppose so." He noted the rectangular outline of a packet of cigarettes in the sheriff's shirt pocket and bit his tongue.

"You won't hear any more about pushing." Winton grinned again. "The kid's father is a fancy lawyer. He's slapping Seven Slopes with a granddaddy of a negligence suit over that loose carpet, so you can bet our baby tumbled all by her little self."

"I see." That explained the photographers, the men

going around asking questions about the carpet, and the newly bared staircase to the bar. He wondered why Winton was still grinning at him.

He took his leave somewhat assured that the investigation was still proceding. But it couldn't bring Anita Soderstrom back, and the Haddad suit shed no light on her death that he could see. He collected his wife from the municipal park where she had been examining the elms for disease, and drove back to Seven Slopes a baffled, angry man.

17

"THE WORLD," DAVIS-WILLIAMS quoted, "stands out on either side, no wider than the heart is wide."

He regarded this new group lugubriously as he read. His own heart felt about the compass of an elderberry; his world knocked at his elbows at every turn, and, if Millay's figure were to be continued, and the sky deemed no higher than his soul, he'd best be careful about turning his nose uppermost, for fear of suffocation.

He could imagine that he looked much the same to this class as he had to the first, only three weeks before, as he stood with his back to the same cold fireplace. He was a little seedier, perhaps, baggier under the eyes, certainly. The same reddish tuft of beard straggled from his chin, the same mostly-British baritone lectured on without his having to think much about it. Even allowing for Dubbins and Falk, mercifully departed with the rest of the earlier batch, and the absence of anyone remotely like The Body, they had little to recommend them. They were, in effect, interchangeable with the remainder of the first group, always excepting Anita Soderstrom: the same distribution in age, the same lack of ability, the same interest chiefly in the university credits that would advance them in their pay scales. With rare insight, he wondered if it might not be better this way. He could settle into harness like the old plow horse he was and plod through the rest of the summer with no great harm done.

Plod he did, while his subconscious mind slowly encapsulated the pain of the last week of June, 1982. The second workshop went by, and the third, with no more excitement than running out of handouts in a meeting or two. There were no more kiln openings: these poets were constrained to understand portraiture and lost-wax casting respectively.

In August, he talked Doris out of driving to western South Dakota to visit the Ammans family—rather more easily than he had anticipated; perhaps their charm had faded in their absence—and they drove instead to the North Shore of Lake Superior, where Doris hunted agates and pointed out the bluebells growing in small cracks in the rocks, although of course she called them *Campanula rotundifolia,* as befitted one who would soon be teaching botany again.

It took September, and a return to the old white frame house on Washburn Avenue where Alonzo the cat waited without perceptible impatience, to crack open the shell around his pain.

Or no. Not the white house on Washburn. The lavender house on Vincent, beside which he parked one afternoon, on a quick trip to the library and Butler Drug.

The switch rolled under Davis-Williams's thumb; the rumble of the typewriter died with a sigh and he blotted the beginning of tears on his shirtsleeve. So. Part One done, again. Had he perhaps lavished too much attention and loving detail upon himself and Anita? Natural enough, given that he felt that he and she were the major figures. Still . . . someone else writing the story—what would he do? Davis-Williams shook his head. Impossible to imagine. As impossible as it was to decide just what it was that made an ordinary man a villain . . .

The yellow cat crouched on the edge of the desk, tail lashing as he stared at something in the budding linden branches beyond the double glass. "Lunch, eh,

Alonzo?'' the poet said. The cat turned, and he saw what the beast had been staring at: a robin. Lunch, indeed!

He'd begin the second half of the book in the morning. Should he skip ahead, perhaps? No. The thing to do was to pick up the tale on that fall day, on the sidewalk outside the lavender house. . . .

PART TWO

18

DAVIS-WILLIAMS MANAGED NOT to recognize the change in himself until he was safely home. Then, leaning against the side door until the lock snapped behind him, he traced the line of a tear down his right cheek with his index finger, smearing it absently side to side as if painting his face. The orange cat came and twined round his ankles, making little chirrupping noises until he stirred, and then it ran ahead of him into the kitchen and stood by its empty dish, miaowing.

Three o'clock. Thursday. Doris would be out until at least quarter past four, teaching the one class she had this trimester, a seminar in the taxonomy of vascular plants. Names. Always names. Davis-Williams pushed the cat out of the way and shook a little Cat Chow into its dish. What was happening to him? He felt—not dizzy, just somehow unconnected to the world.

He walked through the hushed, shaded dining room and up the stairs to his study. At the door he paused, as he often did, to survey what he privately called his kingdom. It was a corner room at the front of the house, with two wide windows linden-tossed, to echo Wilbur, and a bank of floor-to-ceiling bookshelves stuffed with books however they'd fit, most of them worn shabby by his own hands. A fireplace on the inner wall explained the weather-stripping on the door: if Doris was "British" about windows, Davis-Williams was so about fireplaces. In winter, this was often a frigid room with a blazing fire to warm his back.

He had not really thought, until the weather-stripping was in, that it also meant that Doris could put Wagner on the stereo downstairs without his hearing more than the faintest rumor of the bass notes, but that, too, was an advantage. Sounds here, other than the wind in the chimney or the trees, were all his own.

His desk was set between the windows, so that he could look out of either without moving his chair, and to his left, a black metal filing cabinet held his manuscripts, his lesson plans, and, did Doris and the Guggenheim people but know it, the project for which he was to be paid this coming year, all but finished.

The year stretched ahead, as empty as the house. He could type up the book in two days.

Worse, nothing welled in him. Empty year, empty house, empty heart. He crossed to the desk and sat at it and looked out at the lindens, little-leaf lindens whose leaves were hearts as small as his own. His journal had not had a single entry in five weeks. The tape recorder he was in the habit of musing into, so that his thoughts wouldn't have to slow to the pace of his fingers, bore a pale layer of dust. He folded his arms on the desk and put his head down on them and allowed his chest a couple of experimental sobs, but training dies hard and he could feel his upper lip actually stiffen, until the sobs died in a series of tremors. Yet, what else was left?

He wanted to *do* something about Anita Soderstrom. He wanted to make sense of her death. Not excuse it, just make sense of it. That, of course, was Sheriff Winton's job, but Davis-Williams doubted the man had his own urgency, his own need. Still, barring that, what was there?

Doris came into the house, shouting that she had arrived. He must have sat with his mind utterly blank for the better part of an hour: a frightening thought.

168

"I stopped at Lippka's and bought us some lovely shrimp, Owen," she called up the stairs. "Could we broil them out on the back porch?"

"Splendid," he called down to her, consciously putting his mind into gear, so that he could comprehend shrimp, broiling, charcoal. "I'll come start the fire directly." He lumbered to his reluctant feet and down the staircase and into the kitchen, where Doris was already banging cupboard doors in search of the ingredients for one of her marinades; the package from the butcher sat on the counter in its white paper and the cat stretched tall beneath it, pink nose twitching.

"Boot the beast out, would you?" Doris said, without turning to look at him. "Now, where has the Tabasco got to this time?"

"I think I put it on that shelf next to the cooker," Davis-Williams said, picking Alonzo up around the middle and dumping him out the door.

"Why there?" Doris asked, irked. "You *know* I keep it with the spices."

"Not the sauces? It says sauce on the label."

"Yes, but I don't use it that way." She snatched the bottle from the rack where the Kikkoman's and the A-1 lived and shook it violently, as she always did. "Twenty-seven years, Owen," she said. "You'd think in twenty-seven years you'd learn where we keep the Tabasco."

"We've only lived in the house for six," he said, escaping to the garage for charcoal. Not the point, and he knew it, but he didn't feel up to maintaining himself against Doris at the moment.

The idea came to him as he turned the shrimp above the ashy coals. Someone had mentioned a roommate. Yes, the sheriff. A detective had been sent to talk to the roommate. Perhaps the roommate still lived in the same apartment, the garret on Vincent Avenue. And perhaps

169

she'd have some of Anita's poetry, still, there in the apartment. He could choose the best of it and bring out a small book—he had friends, thanks to Guggenheim he had money—one of the local presses would take it, surely Bill Weatherby over at Fine Lines would take it on his recommendation. He'd write an introduction himself. Find a good graphic artist to do the cover. Paperback, of course, he'd want it to sell, the whole idea was that if he couldn't make sense of her death he'd do the next best thing and salvage some of her life.

Pleased with himself, he gave the shrimp more than ordinary care, to Doris's delight. But he didn't tell her about this new project. For one thing, it would make her nag him about his own book, and he'd have to tell her it was already done, and then, who knew what she might find to do with his time?

The apartment mate undoubtedly worked for a living. Saturday afternoon, then, while Doris was at Lund's for the week's groceries, he'd stop by and see if she were in, explain what he wanted to do. He smiled happily.

"What's so wonderful, Owen?"

"The shrimp, love."

"Yes," Doris agreed. "It is rather good, if I say so myself, isn't it?"

19

FRIDAY PASSED IN agony.

After breakfast, he took the manuscript of his sonnet sequence out of its drawer and set it on the desk, just as if he were going to work on it, and dusted off the tape recorder. He uncapped a fresh pen, wrote the date in his journal and stared at it. What to write? All his new enthusiasm, all his excitement was for publishing Anita's work, and he had nothing to write down about that: the idea was bounded in a single sentence. He scarcely needed to remind himself! And that was all. Nothing further he could do, until the next day.

Toward afternoon, he felt that torture with burning bamboo splints under his fingernails might just make time pass a little faster. Even the airplanes that flew low over the house on this cloudy day sounded clumsy and slow, as if time itself were drawn out thick and syrupy, glass ready for the sculptor to shape.

The prospect of his usual evening, reading quietly downstairs with KSJN-FM playing softly in the background, terrified him into inviting Doris to see a film. Her girlish, flattered response at first astounded him. Then he remembered, films in the first years of their marriage, back in the bed-sitter with the shilling meter for the gas fire—Ingmar Bergman so censored as to make no sense, Doris clinging to his arm on the way home, both of them giggling as they filled in the gaps in the plot, his own sharp lust. Where had that gone?

The film, some science-fiction fluff, wasn't sufficiently entertaining to keep Doris from whispering odd chores she'd just remembered into his ear. The contrast with his memories saddened him. Too conscious of mortality, he drove home with all his senses strained against the Friday-night drunk hurtling out of the dark to smash his car, himself. But no such thing happened: he drove up the two concrete ribbons of his driveway to his own garage, comfortable and middle-aged, perfectly safe.

Doris slept late the next morning. That was all right, he told himself, as he paced from one end of his kingdom to the other. The apartment mate probably slept late, too. Be embarrassing to get her out of bed. The ghost of his fantasy of Anita in her velvety dressing gown flitted through his head, and he reddened although no one was there to see him. A mere infatuation, he assured himself, clenching his fists in his pockets. But the poems—there, he felt himself on solid ground. Hadn't he admired them before ever clapping eyes on their author?

He went out to putter in the flower beds, all rather grown up with rover bellflower and quack grass, as one might expect of a border left to itself most of the summer. Chrysanthemums were beginning to bloom, straggly bunches of red and rust and lavender; rudbeckia was nearly done, the tail end of the phlox and a single tardy tiger lily punctuated the line of green beside the drive. A cardinal in the linden in front of the house broke off its song to scratch beneath one wing.

Even birds itch, he thought. Little bugs, lice or mites, lurked under that scarlet cloak, stealing their small portions of the bird's life. Like the thousand daily small annoyances that had stolen his own fresh eye, left him to write as a reflex like the bird's song, an undignified scratching under a wing instead of swift, soaring flight—

Davis-Williams shook his head, not because the metaphor was getting muddled but because he wasn't used to thinking of himself this way. A glimpse of Alonzo stalking some invisible grasshopper or vole reminded him that larger things than lice stole talent, too; impatient to be at work on his new project, he stamped across the tatty lawn waving his arms and hissing *Sssst—scat!* at the astonished cat.

What to do? How to pass a reasonable amount of time?

Too early for the fall garden cleanup. No outlet there for his impatience. He was standing, hands in his hip pockets, contemplating a bed of hosta and wondering if it weren't a trifle sunburned, now that the elm next door had been cut, when Doris called him from the back porch.

They breakfasted on whole-grain toast and a tin of kippers. "That's the last of the fish," he told Doris, hoping to hurry her along. Wouldn't it be ironic if the apartment mate decided to shop at the same time? He could just see it—Doris and Cary (or would it be Carrie, or Kari?) Ellis queued at the same cash register, while he pounded futilely at the door at the top of those outside stairs.

While Doris cleaned up the kitchen he went out and fidgeted at the weeds. A cloud came over the sun. He hoped it wasn't an omen.

"I'm off to the grocery, Owen," Doris said at last, emerging from the house with the car keys in hand.

"Want me to come?" he asked, as usual. Wouldn't do to depart from habit.

"Dear heaven, no," Doris said, as always. "You'd buy up the entire shop. It's getting chilly, don't you think?" she added, with a glance at the curdled sky. "I think I'll take a jacket, after all."

He followed her into the house before she could begin nagging and pulled a battered old sweater over his head, a sweater Doris had knit years before of "good, British

173

wool," his mother had sent. Threads of her blond hair were caught in with the dark blue yarn here and there, proving that she had paid more attention to what she had been reading as she knit than to the simple stitch of the pattern. He pulled at a couple of the light loops without result.

"More gardening?" she asked.

"I thought I might take a walk."

"If you wait until I'm done shopping, I'll come with you."

"More gardening, then," he agreed mildly, and picked the hoe up from its nest beside the back steps in case she glanced at him while backing the car down the drive. He gave her five minutes to return for something forgotten, and when she didn't reappear, he set out.

The lavender house sat close to the sidewalk and was surrounded by a badly weathered picket fence choked with weeds. The fence had once been white, and sometime over the past summer someone had made a small effort at clearing the weeds and scraping old paint, but had given up after six or seven boards. The outside staircase was reached by its own cracked concrete path and had its own gate in the fence. He stepped through the gate and latched it behind him, unconsciously looking about for a dog. But none came barking after him, and he mounted the roofed staircase trailing his left hand along the top of the half wall that served as an outside handrail. The treads needed paint, and the inside of the half wall was the same sickly green the house had been before its recent lavender transformation.

Deep breath. Tap at the door.

After an interval long enough to set him wondering if perhaps his idea about the supermarket had been a premonition rather than a simple qualm, a sleepy, bearded face appeared at the crack of the door. Davis-

Williams stepped back involuntarily. A *male* apartment mate?

"Um?" said the bearded face.

"Er, my name is Owen Davis-Williams," he said. A gray tiger-striped cat squeezed through the slim opening of the door and streaked down the steps. He made a grab, far too late.

"Rum!" shouted the beard.

"I say, I am sorry," Davis-Williams stammered, startled back to Britain by the single syllable.

"Rum, come back here!" shouted the beard. The cat had vanished into a clump of mildewed lilacs and the absolute silence of the branches indicated that it was crouching, wary. "That's all right," the man assured Davis-Williams. "He'll be back in a minute. He always thinks he's on the wrong side of the door. What did you want?"

So, Rum was the cat's name. Davis-Williams stuttered out his purpose, encouraged by nods and rumbles from the beard. "So I wondered," he finished, "whether any of her poems might be here? So that some of it could be published, as sort of, er—"

"Oh, sure," the man said. "I got you." Davis-Williams felt the same sense of cool appraisal from these brown eyes as Anita had sometimes given him. "Only there's not very much. She got rid of a lot just before she went to Seven Slopes. You can look at what's left, if you want. Come on in."

The door opened wider and Davis-Williams followed the beard into the room. He was wearing a dressing gown, a deep red one that raised the hairs on the back of Davis-Williams's neck, and his feet were bare. "My name's Cary Ellis," he said.

A small black and white cat lay on its side on one of the two chairs in the room, industriously washing between its toes, and resisted Ellis's gentle shove without even pausing in its bath. "Out, Jelly," Ellis commanded.

The cat gave Davis-Williams a brief glance he was sure had been designed to haunt him the rest of his days and moved onto the floor. Davis-Williams claimed the chair, well warmed by a good, long lie-in on the part of the cat. The cat continued its bath at his feet, loudly and thoroughly.

"Coffee?"

"Yes, thank you, if it's no trouble."

"Just made some."

The room rose to a flattened point in the center, with four large sections of slanted ceiling, each pierced by a big dormer facing one of the cardinal points. Ellis stepped into the east dormer, which had been fitted out as a kitchen, and returned carrying two large mugs. "What do you take in it?" he asked.

"A little milk, if you have it."

"Sure." The chap had been domesticated, anyone could see that. He looked in his late thirties, dark-haired and dark-eyed, well built but a trifle stooping, although that might have been the effect of the ceiling. Davis-Williams searched the one cozy room for evidence of Anita but saw none, unless he counted the photo portrait of her that stood on one of the bookshelves. The books were few and technical. Had her own books gone, then? Already?

He steadied the mug while Ellis poured milk into it straight from the carton. "The police were here, asking if she knew anybody up there before she went," Ellis said. "There wasn't one single name I recognized."

She had died among strangers. A question occurred to Davis-Williams for the first time, not only about Anita Soderstrom, but also about all of those summer students, hundreds by now: "Why did she go?"

"She said she felt stale." The man stared into his mug.

"She could have taken her vacation with me, like always," he burst out. "I wanted to see the Pacific Northwest, hike in the Cascades, but she—" He lapsed into silence.

"Stale?"

"She said she was pulled apart, couldn't write, too—something—the job, me, I don't know. I never understood."

"Her art, man, her art!"

"Art?" Ellis turned his large brown eyes toward the bookshelves. "Her poems, you mean? She burned them . . . some of them. There aren't all that many." He looked about. "It's not that much of a place to keep up."

Davis-Williams followed his thought perfectly, effortlessly. Now, examining the room more closely, he saw that a plant hanging in a basket over the kitchen sink was quite dead, that a beer can lay barely in sight under the brick and board bookshelves, an irregular gray line beside what he supposed was a divan showed that a vacuum cleaner had been applied only recently after long disuse. She *was* still in the room, then, or rather, her absence was.

"She needed encouragement," he said.

Ellis regarded him quietly. Again, he felt himself being evaluated, perhaps as a rival? The man seemed to come to a decision, although what faint alteration of his face revealed it, Davis-Williams couldn't say.

"I can lend you this, if you're sure to return it," Ellis said. He carried his mug past what Davis-Williams now recognized as a bed fitted with a dark sheet and a tumbled comforter and set it down on top of the bookshelves. Davis-Williams averted his gaze from the bed. Ellis took a black loose-leaf notebook from the bottom shelf. "It's got some poems in it."

Davis-Williams reached for the notebook. Quite fat,

he saw, becoming excited again. He flipped open the cover: there was "The Maiden Aunt." His eyes squeezed themselves shut. She'd been writing about someone else, someone he'd never know. His hands closed the notebook. Ellis, this one room—how had she fooled him like that?

"I'd appreciate the use of it," he said, opening his eyes. "I can do a good job on a collection of poems. I've done four of my own."

"Yeah, I heard."

"I'll give you my phone number—I live just over on Washburn—if you happen to find anything else?"

"Sure."

He finished his coffee, making little spurts of small talk, refused the offer of more, got up clasping the notebook to his chest. When he got to the door he saw that the black and white cat had already jumped into the chair and was aggressively washing its ears. Did it miss her? he wondered. Not bloodly likely. No more than Alonzo missed him, or Doris, when they were gone and the neighbors were feeding him.

When the door opened, the other cat shot through it into the house. "What'd I tell you?" Ellis asked, bending to scratch the beast's ears.

Davis-Williams trudged homeward still hugging the black notebook to his chest, shaken. He'd been deceived! No, he had let himself be deceived. Thud of his crepe-soled shoes on pavement. Oh, all right! He'd deceived himself, read more into "The Maiden Aunt" than could possibly have been warranted; her intelligence, air of self-containment, reticence, maybe even her pallor— all of this had melded with the confusion of his *middle-age crisis!*—how disgustingly bourgeois!—into a picture of her as alone, virgin, an observer from the sidelines of life, like himself.

A child drifting past on a bike tossed an empty pop

can into the gutter, and he barely looked up. He'd been wrong. Asininely wrong. She had a life apart from her poems, as who did not? She'd loved that oaf Ellis, lived with him, taken him . . . he flushed as he remembered his fantasy of introducing her to her own body . . . she was human . . . didn't that make her the more worthy of his remembrance? Braver?

And Ellis just as likely not an oaf . . . must still be grieving . . . the photograph, sterile studio photograph but the face was hers, the smile her little smile that touched her eyes first . . . she had perhaps been secretive? The man must have qualities that drew her to him (Don't think of the bed! Don't think of the bed!), despite his lack of appreciation of her poetry. Or did he not appreciate it? Had she not appreciated her poems herself? A deep shame came over him, in the form of a painful flush that stopped him dead in his tracks. *The New York Times Book Review* had praised his poems for their sensitivity, had they not? And *American Book Review?* All those gratifying little notes from editors, had they all been wrong, after all?

He started walking again, shuffling little steps like an old man's, holding the notebook as if it were a life ring thrown to him as he floundered out of his depth.

The trip hadn't taken long. The car wasn't in the drive. He let himself into the house and carried the notebook up to his kingdom, afraid to look into it again. He set it down in the center of his desk and stared at it. Now what?

A few minutes later Doris hollered for help with the groceries. He went gladly down to fetch the brown bags from the boot of the car. The necessity of pretending all was well, that he had puttered in the garden and then gone to his study to polish words, broke the mood that had come upon him. As he unpacked cans and handed them to Doris to stow away, some of the excitement of the previous day began to rebuild.

He could scarcely believe he had won such a prize. The black binder was fat, fat, fat, the edges of the pages encouragingly worn. There must be, he calculated rapidly, a couple of hundred poems in his hands. Sixty of the best would make a wholly respectable volume.

He flipped "The Maiden Aunt" aside without looking at it and began to read, cheered by finding his three sonnets, the ones she had sent ahead. Twelve good poems, so far, he gloated a few minutes later. And then—

Scribbled workshop pages. His own handwriting leaped out at him. *Good, good!* in red ink, all over the place. Nothing but *good, good!* Everywhere, *good, good!* He came close to tears again: she'd never have renewed herself from this! He'd done her the same disservice he complained of himself, comments that were always praising, never faintly critical.

Not one more poem. Those twelve only, and four or five from the workshop. Four or five, because one was a very good start, a good start indeed, almost a poem as it stood, but she had not yet cast it into verse.

Perhaps had never intended to?

But, sixteen short poems! Slim, even for a chapbook. The rest of the fat notebook was only journal. He pouted as he began to scan the minute, controlled script.

A moment later he found himself chuckling. The journal seemed to begin with the bus trip north. Here was The Body, name unknown but unmistakably Roz, posturing her way onto the bus: "A child with a doe's soft face, fiercely attempting cougarhood." The Body sat beside a farmer and poured poetical comments at him— Davis-Williams laughed aloud—for ten miles before the farmer turned the tables and began discussing feeder pigs and the feasibility of using potato peels as feed. Could the chap really have maintained that the fad for french-fried potato peels would raise pork prices, or was that Anita having someone on?

Here was Sue Falk, by name. Davis-Williams paused and stared out the window at the nearest linden branch. Did that mean Anita had already known her? And "Miriam—she permits me to call her *Mim*—Dubbins." That had the ring of recent introduction. What could that asterisk mean?

He shuffled through a couple of pages and found the matching asterisk. The bus station. Conversation between Sue and Mim and Anita. "Lord," he murmured. "Someone should have told her where Miriam published her poems." He stopped reading at a tap on the door. "Owen?" Doris shouted through the white-painted panel. "Ready for supper?"

"Down in a moment," he called back. Reluctantly, he closed the journal and put it into one of the desk drawers. He'd read the rest after supper.

He woke in the early hours of the morning and lay still in the warm bed. A storm had come up with the shadow of darkness, and now he listened to the rain lashing the house and the clematis vine on the trellis outside scratching at the wall as if it wanted to come in. Gradually, an idea formed: something he could do. With his sonnet sequence already completed, he could spend most of his time on anything, up in his kingdom with the door shut, and neither Doris nor Guggenheim the wiser. He'd spend that time writing about Anita's last days on earth, and hope thereby to make some sense of her early death.

He'd make it like a murder mystery, one of those concoctions Doris was always reading. Davis-Williams smiled into the dark at the irony of writing what Doris loved and couldn't read. He'd have to fudge some of it, that was clear. Depend upon his intuition, make up things that might have gone on when neither he nor Anita was present, that kind of thing. Write it all up as if he'd known it all, all the time.

He could do better. He could write to the other students on some sort of pretext, get their journals for that week. Plenty of material there, probably, in among the lists of wildflowers and the candle meditations. Surely he could depend upon amateur journals to have turned into diaries? He rolled over in bed and groped for the pencil always ready to hand on his night table. "Journals," he wrote on the small notepad that also lay ready, and turned the page for the next note.

A car went past the house, and the lights traveled across the ceiling in the opposite direction, a mystery he had never quite figured out. Where to begin this roman à clef?

The temptation was to start with his own first experience, with those exquisite poems that had fallen out of his mail that late May morning. No, that wouldn't do, he could see that. Better begin with Anita, just where she had begun herself, in the downtown bus station, waiting to catch the bus to Coleridge. . . .

Yes. Satisfied, he reached out and scribbled "bus" on the notepad, without turning on the lamp or disturbing the even rhythm of his wife's breathing.

Sue Falk and Miriam Dubbins. He could just see Sue in that idiot T-shirt, binding against her fat neck and under her fat arms because she'd put it on backward. But Anita! The woman noticed everything, and wrote it all down! What to put in, what to leave out? The gray-and-black-chequered tile of the bus station floor, or only the drying puddles of spilled pop? The iridescent green of the puddles, or only their stickiness? The stinking bag lady asleep with her mouth slack, and Anita watching to see if the fly on her cheek would crawl onto her tongue, or only the poets?

A novelization. It seemed an ordinary thing, with problems akin to those of poetry, problems he could work out while pacing from one end of his Heriz rug to the other. Certainly not a thing to endanger life or limb.

Gradually, the rain settled down to a steady soaking, the clematis resigned itself to life on a trellis, and Davis-Williams joined his wife in snoring peacefully in the hushed room.

20

Sunday.

With the eagerness and haste with which he approached any new project, Davis-Williams spent the whole of a fine September afternoon up in his study, examining Anita's journal.

He had few illusions about the difficulty of the task he had set himself. Never a fiction writer, he had listened at the edge of many a discussion of the art of fiction writing and had counted himself lucky that poetry shared only the problems of sound, sense, and pacing, and didn't often burden itself with plot or characterization. But he did fully believe the old canard about a novelist being a failed poet, and wasn't he already a poet? Further, he had the advantage of writing about real places and real people; his powers of invention could scarcely be taxed under those circumstances! He hoped, further, that his own extensive reading had percolated into his subconscious sufficiently to give him some style; he knew that he could construct a grammatical sentence when so called upon, and he knew also that it was his one great talent to describe. That some critics had accused him of "adjectivitis" he considered proof of a nature so arrogant that it thought it could divine his meaning from the barest evidence. How should they know whether he meant a sky to be gray or blue, if he didn't say?

After a great deal of thought, he got out one of the dozen yellow legal pads he had bought, years before, when someone had told him it was fashionable to write on such pads while waiting to change planes at O'Hare. He had found it impossible to write poetry on such a bilious color, and had changed planes at O'Hare only twice in all the years since, but at least Guggenheim wouldn't have to pay for materials for his under-the-table novel.

He headed the first page "Sunday Afternoon," and under that wrote: Anita's Journal. Bus. Arrival. Registration.

By the time Doris called him to dinner, he had listed the incidents from his own journal, such as it was, and Anita's, interleaving them in chronological order. Not everything Anita said made sense. What could she have meant by, "Surprise: Martin teaches ceramics. Importunate, but under control."? Knowing the man goaded his curiosity, but he had to remain unsatisfied. Other entries were, if possible, even more obscure. He skipped them.

Wide gaps in the tale remained. Some of them he could fill in from his own memory. For the rest, he would have to hope for help from the other poets.

"You are working hard," Doris commented. "Why, when you have a whole year to get this book done?"

"Oh, I had a new idea about how to organize the book," he replied, honestly if obliquely. "I thought I'd like to try it out."

"You missed some splendid weather. I stopped down at the lake. Some green herons there."

"Which lake?" Doris had whipped up some eggs; she poured them into the hot omelet pan and began to shake it. Davis-Williams thought he had smelled mushrooms frying; he hoped they were to go into the omelet.

"Calhoun." Doris scattered he-couldn't-quite-see-what onto the eggs. "Oh, I met one of your students, jogging around the lake. He said to say hello."

Only a fellow from the summer's last workshop, it turned out, but there was another thought: he could interview people, ask questions. His stomach quivered at the thought of asking questions of Dubbins and/or Falk, but this, he supposed, was the sort of thing writers of things other than poetry had to put up with from time to time. His earlier notion of fudging the empty spots had disappeared without his taking notice: now, he wanted the strictest accuracy, and spooned Doris's velvety chocolate mousse into his mouth without really tasting it, although it was one of his favorite sweets.

The next morning, Monday, he walked over to the print shop behind the Tom Thumb store and had them run off twenty copies of his request for the use of the journal entries. He had labored over the wording as over the construction of a sestina, hoping for replies from all the students.

In the afternoon he folded the letters into envelopes, stamped them, addressed them from his class list, and carried them down to the mailbox by the drug store. Now, all he could do was wait.

As an afterthought, he wrote a different letter to Sheriff Winton, asking whether there had been any progress in the investigation.

His first reply came Friday afternoon, in the form of a phone call from the sheriff. He took it in the hall downstairs, where he could keep an eye on Doris to see how closely she was eavesdropping.

"What are you up to, Williams?" Winton demanded.

Doris slammed the back door. A moment later he saw her attacking spent flower stalks in the back perennial border with a pair of secateurs.

"I'm writing a book."

"God help us!"

"I've published four others," Davis-Williams said severely. No need to mention that they were all verse. "I'm not an amateur."

"What kind of book d'you have in mind?"

Davis-Williams explained his project, nettled by the sheriff's occasional chuckle. He described it as something still in the first stages of thought; no mention of the letters he had sent the others. The sheriff, he imagined, might find the idea overly bold.

"Look," the man said. "You've got no idea what you're doing. What can you expect to learn from two diaries? Just to give you an idea, when we were digging into her background we found out that she worked as a waitress at Seven Slopes one summer, twelve years ago. But," the sheriff sighed, "the only one left from then is Peletier, who thought she was snubbing him, so he didn't bother to remind her that he knew her."

"What about that?" Davis-Williams interrupted. "Would that incite him?"

"To *murder?*" Winton paused. "Pretty farfetched, if you ask me. 'Specially for a guy like Peletier, who's an even-tempered old coot. Besides, he's an Indian, they're used to insults."

Davis-Williams blinked at this casual dismissal of the man's feelings and decided, regretfully, that Winton was probably right.

"Anyway, I was telling you about the scope of an investigation like this. I got a girl doing nothing but checking out old guest lists against who was there this summer. I'm talking to everybody who might have seen her in Coleridge when she went into town to buy a half dozen doughnuts. You know she took two years of ceramics at the U a few years back? I'm checking potters."

"I don't think it was a potter," Davis-Williams objected, seizing upon the one piece of information he could digest instantly. "Unless it was Carlotta Mc-Cready."

"No?"

"Who would deliberately ruin someone else's work? When he could simply fling the knife into the bushes?"

"Who knows? People do weird things. Anyway, the point is, you don't have anything to write about, much less a book. So stick to your sonnets and make Mr. Guggenheim happy."

Davis-Williams drew back his chin and stared at the telephone, which chuckled. "I can write it from the other angle," he insisted. "I can ask the other students to help me piece it together."

"I wouldn't do that, Mr. Williams," the sheriff said. "You could get yourself in a lot of trouble that way."

His stomach tingled and sank. "What do you mean?"

"You're looking at a murder," Sheriff Winton reminded him. "Don't forget, where there's been a murder, there has to be a murderer."

"Yes, quite, but—"

"Motive and opportunity, Mr. Williams. Motive and opportunity. And a determined man can always make an opportunity. Don't give a motive if you can help it."

"I see."

"And if you've already been dumb enough to give a motive, you better make damn sure you don't give an opportunity."

"Yes. I see." Doris had bundled up the spent perennial stalks and cast them on the compost heap, and now came at an angle across the lawn toward the house. "Was there anything else, sheriff?" he asked. "Because I'm rather busy."

"Nope," Winton said. "Enjoy your Guggenheim."

The line clicked and buzzed, and Davis-Williams slowly replaced the receiver. So. His own background had also been investigated, and without his even being aware of it. Chilling thought.

The back door banged open and Doris came into the hall, where he still stood beside the telephone. "What did he want?" she asked. "Not more trouble over that unfortunate girl, I hope?"

"No. Just a point or two he wanted to clarify."

"Dreadful, that he should interrupt your work," Doris complained, returning to the kitchen. "People in this country have no respect for the arts, poetry in particular."

"It won't kill me to talk to someone once in a while," he said, following her. "Shall we go out to dinner tonight for a change?"

"Oh, lovely," Doris said. "We haven't done that in nearly a month. Where shall we go?"

Operation Distraction successful.

The next response to his letters was also a telephone call, which he answered himself while Doris was doing the Saturday shopping.

"It's Rozlynne Haddad," the caller said, when he had identified himself. Her voice was different, more childish in timbre than he remembered, but with an overlay of maturity that struck him as new.

"Ah, yes, Miss Haddad."

"It's about that letter you sent." Her voice shifted to the low, pleasant tone he was used to. "I don't have a journal, but I want to talk to you about that—that time. In person, if I can."

Warily, he said: "I suppose a meeting could be arranged. Somewhere for coffee, perhaps?"

"Well." She sounded embarrassed. "I can't go out by myself, because of, you know, the accident. So, if you could come here—"

Come, come you're a grown man of some experience,

he chided himself. Surely you have nothing to fear from a girl of twenty! "Where's here?"

"I'm back living with my parents." He hoped she hadn't heard his involuntary sigh of relief. "It's out near Lake Minnetonka. You'd have to drive."

"I'll have the car Tuesday afternoon," he said, thinking of Doris's teaching schedule. "Would that be convenient?"

"Any time is convenient for me," she said wistfully. "Why don't you come out around three, and my mother will be here to let you in?"

"That sounds good," he said. Especially the bit about the mother. He'd fix the car with Doris, plead—what? Dentist. Always having trouble with his teeth. Dentist was a good one.

So convincing did he find this excuse to be that when he had hung up, he very nearly called the dentist for an appointment.

He thought he had enough material in Anita's journal to get a one-chapter start on the book. He was shocked, on sitting down to it the next afternoon, at how difficult it was to begin. He tried the old trick of a poem, beginning before the beginning, to write the kinks out of his brain, but it didn't work.

At last he tried reading Anita's journal into his ancient reel-to-reel tape recorder, as he often did his poems. Listening to the mass of description, he wrote down what struck him most. Better, better. Bones to hang some flesh upon. Sentences to shape. A paragraph to break apart, put back together. The thought that what he was doing was a species of plagiarism never entered his head.

By Monday morning, he had fallen into the method of working he was to adopt for the rest of the book: he read what he had written the day before into the tape recorder, listened to his own voice saying the words as he followed along in the manuscript, and then marked the difficulties, the necessary revisions, and typed it all up. Out of the habit of his poems he made a carbon copy for his files. The first copy, the working copy, he shoved into his center desk drawer.

Monday's mail brought a Xerox of a journal from Dorothy LaBruyere. Parts had been blacked out with a marking pen: heavy, forbidding lines that made him want to peep behind them. She had written a sweet, rose-scented little note much like her sweet, white-haired and rose-scented little self, that fired him with curiosity. What could she possibly have noted down to warrant such decisive censorship? He was to use the journals however he wished and then discard them, she wrote; the workshop had been of inestimable value; she hoped to attend again next summer.

"Absolute imbecility," he muttered, and applied himself to trying to read behind the black lines.

He could do so quite easily, he discovered, simply by holding the sheet of paper to the sunlight and tilting it so that the light glanced off the heavier ink of the copy. "A lascivious young woman in training to be a whore," he read. Roz again! She couldn't say she made no impression on people. Women, at least. What would the men have to say about her? McCready? Saarinen? Davis-Williams pressed his lips together. ". . . Pursued the instructor from one side of the room to the other, an inch at a time, while he, a young man with a strange growth of hair on his chin, continually sidled away."

Davis-Williams tugged at his beard and guffawed. He must remember, should he ever care to censor something, to do his crossing out on a copy and make another from it. He hoped none of his other students would think of so unobvious a subterfuge. But, young! A *young* man!

While the sun shone he made hay by writing out the

blackened bits of Dorothy's delectable diary. Time enough to fill them in on the empty spaces of his legal pad when the sun had dropped behind the house across the street.

Tuesday afternoon, moaning with what he thought was tolerable authenticity, he drove his wife to her class in St. Paul and zipped back across the Mississippi on I-94 with a pounding heart. He negotiated the transition to U.S. 12 with a feeling of unreality: most often, he came this way at rush hour, and to drive the route at the speed limit gave him an almost frightening sense of power.

Past Golden Valley he was in seldom-visited territory; the sides of the road had been built up more than he remembered, and the buildings had less the raw concrete look he recalled and more of a gloss on them. Gradually even these gave way to sweeps of marshland clotted with late-blooming purple loosestrife, and to an occasional pasture, one dotted with real cows.

In Wayzata, the narrow highway became lined with trees. Roz's directions had been detailed and precise. He had no difficulty in choosing where to leave the highway, or in winding through back roads with clusters of mailboxes at their intersections; he arrived without a single wrong turn at a crossroads with a signpost on which the names of homeowners were painted, with arrows pointing, as Roz had promised, toward their homes. Only three pointed toward the lake. Haddad was the second.

The approach to the house slipped through undisturbed woodland. What must it cost to plow this drive each winter? Davis-Williams wondered. A gray squirrel chattered in a tree as he passed beneath it, a chipmunk darted across the drive; there were surely deer among the rough trunks of the oaks.

He was thinking, Doris-like, how different this was

from the woods at Seven Slopes when he rounded a bend and came upon the house.

The Haddads were clearly out of his class. Not that the house was imposing at first glance: fieldstone and shingle, it blended perfectly with the trees around it. Only when he thought of the architect's fees, the difficulty of bringing in the materials, how carefully it must have been nestled here, did he realize just how much money he was looking at.

The impression continued as he parked his old clunker on the immaculate gravel lot beside the house and approached the front entrance along a planter in which literally thousands of late marigolds and zinnias thrived without a weed among them. The pungent odor of the marigolds hung in the air as if shielding the house against him as he stopped to admire the hand-carving of the door before pressing the bell.

He half expected the door to be opened by a butler, but it swung inward in the hand of a woman who could only be Rozlynne Haddad's mother. She had the same dark curls and oval face, although the perfect complexion was marred by a mole on one cheek from which four or five dark hairs sprouted. Her eyes were the same shining brown. She cocked her head at him without saying a word.

"I'm Owen Davis-Williams," he said, feeling rather like a schoolboy sent to the headmaster's office by a teacher exasperated beyond endurance.

"Yes. Come in." Her voice was warm and velvety, as her daughter's would be in another twenty years, and although she must be nearly as old as Doris, his confident prediction that figures like The Body's ran to fat past thirty was emphatically proven wrong. Not that she dressed like her daughter: the beige linen dress was, if anything, more conservative than he might have expected to see on a woman in her own home on a warm late September afternoon. That she might have dressed up to meet a well-known author did not occur to him.

He advanced into a tile-floored entry that opened onto a living room that would have contained two of Anita's small flat. As he did so, Rozlynne appeared from another part of the house and came toward him, balanced on two gleaming chrome crutches that angled to support her forearms. The lovely long legs were in braces, the proud young feet in sensible flat-heeled shoes that laced and were tied with a double knot in the bow.

"You can look at me," she said, "I don't mind."

Without makeup, she looked very young, much younger than he had taken her for that summer. He could think of nothing to say.

"Let's go out on the deck," she said. "That way." She used a jerk of her head to point, just as had another of his students, who had been crippled by polio as a small child; the gesture dismayed him almost more than the clicking braces and crutches.

Somehow an introduction to her mother had been made, he had engaged in a brief, warm handclasp, and was following Roz through the tiled hall and onto a deck poised above the brim of the lake, beside which a blue swimming pool seemed utterly superfluous.

She saw him looking at the pool. "I spend a lot of time in there," she remarked. "Holding on to the side and kicking. Keeps my legs from going to pot."

"I'm sorry to see you like this," he said.

Roz grinned. Even without lipstick, her lips were pink and well defined. "You ain't half as sorry as me."

"I'm sure."

"Sit down," she said.

He perched on the edge of one of the chairs she pointed at, again with her chin: some sort of green metal chair with bright flower-print cushions the colors of the marigolds and zinnias tied into it. A moment later Mrs.

Haddad appeared with a tray bearing a pitcher of iced tea and two tall glasses. She set it on a small table near his elbow.

"Do you mind pouring?" she asked. "Rozlynne can't, and she wants me to leave you alone."

Alone, but not unwatched. The back of the house, its eyes and heart, faced the lake. He chatted a moment with the mother, poured out some tea and offered Roz sugar and lemon, of which she took only the sugar. "Do you mind my asking," he began, and foundered before the phrase was done.

"How bad it is?" She tossed her head in lieu of a shrug. "It's sort of permanent and sort of not. I'll be able to walk again, probably, if I work real hard at it, but I'll always have to be careful of my back. I don't think I'll do much dancing," she added wistfully. "Not like I used to."

To be twenty, and never dance again! His mind skittered toward other activities, what he'd read in Anita's journal, and to cover his confusion he said, "You were a good dancer, too, I've heard." Oh, wrong thing! he thought.

"Crazy, I think," she said without evident offense. She put the glass of tea down. "Now's when I want a cigarette," she complained. "They made me quit in the hospital. I guess it's good for me in the long run, but damn it, it's hard."

"I know." The conversation was slithering away from him, somehow; he didn't know how to turn it to what he wanted; in the face of this gleaming metal, these laced leather supports, the crutches so carefully placed beside the chair, how could he talk about another woman's death?

A little breeze smelling of fish came off the lake, where a sailboat had just come about and stood in the water with mainsail flapping. He heard the snap as the wind

195

filled the sail again, some music—Vivaldi?—from the house behind him.

"I keep trying to figure it out," Roz said.

"How you fell?"

Her face shifted, unreadable. "No. Who killed Anita. That's what your letter was about, wasn't it? I mean, what it was really about? You want our journals so you can figure it out?"

He nodded. Had it been so transparent as that?

"You weren't the only one with the hots for Anita, you know," Roz said. "That guy—what the hell was his name? Jeez, three months and it's like half my life ago. You know, the blood-flowers-blooming guy?"

"Moose."

"Yeah, Moose. He was after her, I mean, he just wouldn't leave her *alone,* and that guy that taught the pottery thing."

"Not Martin!"

"That's right, Martin. She slept with him before, for over a year, she said. God, I wish I knew what she had. That guy was *frantic!*"

"Good heavens," Davis-Williams said, inadequately. "Still, do you think either of them would have killed her? One does meet with rejection quite regularly, without becoming . . . murderously frustrated."

A lopsided smile flickered over her mouth. "If they really *cared,* maybe? Otherwise, the only thing I can think of is, it must have been a mistake. Or maybe she saw something she shouldn't have seen. Like maybe she really did see something about that burglary, that first night? Or maybe she saw somebody she knew there, that wasn't supposed to be there?"

"I'd think she would have put it in her journal."

"Yeah, I know, but there was lots of stuff she didn't put in her journal. Like she wrote a letter to her boyfriend that was, uh, what they call explicit—I read it—

196

wow, did she have ideas!—but she never once mentioned him in that journal.''

Davis-Williams repressed the twinge of desire that had hit him at the word *ideas* and refocused on what Roz had just said. ''You read her journal, too?''

''Shameless, that's me,'' she said, with an impish glimmer of her old grin, and sobered instantly.

''Did she know?''

Roz regarded him warily. ''No, I don't think so,'' she said, much of the vibrancy leaving her voice.

''I've also read Anita's journal, Miss Haddad. I know, ah, why you attended the workshop.''

Roz flushed. ''I was such a kid! I've got a whole new head, now. They sent me to a shrink.'' Her eyes followed the sailboat as it came about again. She can't sail, either, Davis-Williams thought. ''You won't tell my mother, will you?'' she asked suddenly.

He almost laughed. She looked so very earnest! ''I can't begin to imagine such a conversation, Miss Haddad,'' he assured her.

She sighed and shifted in the chair, still very straight. The edge of a brace briefly tightened the loose fabric of her dress. ''Call me Roz, can't you?'' she asked. ''I get nervous being Miss Haddad. It's like I'm my Aunt Rima, and she's—'' Roz made a face.

''Quite,'' he replied, feeling inane.

''What did you want from me?'' Roz asked. ''Just a general idea? Or some specific question?''

So the ball was in his court, and he watched it dribble away, metaphorically speaking. ''Just memories,'' he said. ''Or maybe you could apply your feminine intuition, to the, ah, events, and come up with, ah . . . ''

''It's only men who go on and on about feminine intuition,'' Roz said petulantly. She sipped at her iced tea and put it down, very straight and careful. He noticed that she no longer licked her lips in that way that had annoyed him so, and wondered if the lipstick had been uncomfortable. "Men don't have intuition," she continued. "Just hunches. Or gut feelings, yeah. You guys always have to have your guts on the line."

He flipped his hands by way of apology.

"But . . . I don't know . . . about intuition . . . another idea I've had is, what if something was funny about the room? That we shared?"

"You mean because you both . . . but surely, such different injuries?"

The girl shuddered. She looked out over the swimming pool, lower lip sucked in.

"Sheriff Winton said, after you fell, that you told him I pushed you," Davis-Williams blurted. "I hope you don't believe that. I tried to catch you, truly I did. I was horrified to feel you slip, I—"

"He said that?" Roz exclaimed.

Davis-Williams stopped talking.

"I never said you pushed me."

"But you were pushed?" he asked without thinking, impelled by something in her tone.

Her face went blank. "There's a negligence action, you know," she reminded him. "I shouldn't talk to you about that at all, my father would just kill me."

He had totally forgotten the lawsuit. He must have looked shocked, because she said, "Just an expression. I just didn't think."

He smiled to reassure her. "It doesn't make any difference. Oh, my turn! I meant, I don't think it has any bearing on Anita's death."

"On her murder, Professor," she corrected, turning those dark eyes full upon him. "Anita was murdered. She was a perfectly decent person, and she got murdered. Don't you forget it."

*　　*　　*

198

Odd, he mused, as he drove homeward along the gradually widening highway, that both of the people he had talked to had thought it necessary to remind him that Anita had been murdered. Why else was he writing this book? Why else would he seek them out?

She had worn that dress, the dress she had died in, once before, the wide hem swirling as she walked. Don't think of it, he warned himself. Don't think of it.

The hem swirling, the pale slender legs, the brown sandals, downcast eyes and an inward, musing smile.

Don't. You'll cry.

Slim, pale arms. The lightest dusting of freckles. An odor of sun lotion. The tilt of her head, a mirror of Doris's at breakfast that last morning. Had she been merely polite, when he'd thought she was interested? In what he had to say, in *him?* He blushed as he remembered his lecherous visions, and had them again.

"But she's dead!" he wailed at the windshield. "She's dead! What kind of mind do you have, you old satyr, that keeps wanting her back?"

A red light stopped him. He breathed deeply, through his nose, willing his heart to slow. Loud punk rock came through the open window: he bathed his jangling nerves in it, to give them a reason to jangle. Traffic was getting heavier in the waning afternoon. The attention it claimed helped to calm him. Still time to change plans and pick Doris up after her seminar. No. Let her come home on the bus, as planned. He needed time. . . .

He found the familiar progression of the roads as he neared home soothing, and dared to look again into his memories of Anita. How virginal she had seemed, how pure! What was it he had needed from her, to misunderstand her so completely? Or was it that he thought she needed him, as Doris had once done, that he needed another life to run . . . She'd slept with Martin! Martin! Martin of such long acquaintance, whose mousy wife had always seemed to be adequate, even appropriate, to him. . . . A chill ran down his spine. Martin, the one man who could control who put the pots into the kiln.

He put the car away and let himself into the house. Doris, to his relief, was not yet home. What sort of dental work should he say he'd had done? More root canal? No, too fancy. Tangled web, that. He pacified Alonzo with some Cat Chow and retreated to his kingdom, where some of the linden leaves had already turned golden and the fireplace had begun to stink of last year's smoke.

"Look at you," he said to his reflection in the mirror over the mantel. "What kind of man are you, with your secrets?" Secrets from everyone, most particularly himself. Seized with a sudden desire to see his own face, he went into the bathroom and shaved off his beard.

He heard Doris arrive as he contemplated his newly bared chin. Odd. He'd almost forgotten that faint cleft, slightly off center, that had seemed so glaringly asymmetrical when he was seventeen.

"Owen, are you home?" Doris called. "Oh, hell. He'll never hear me with that bloody door shut," he heard her mutter, and the stairs creaking as she hurried up them. He stepped out of the bathroom to greet her.

"Eeek!"

Doris backed slowly down three steps, her eyes wide, before saying, "Owen, what have you done?"

"I've shaved my beard."

"Why?"

"I wondered what I looked like." He ran his right hand over his raw chin. "Not so bad, hmmm?"

"No-o-o-o," she said uncertainly. "You might have warned me. I thought someone had broken in."

"I didn't know I was going to do it myself, until just a bit ago," he explained. "Just an irresistible impulse."

* * *

She continued to glance doubtfully at him from time to

200

time while he helped her cook dinner and set the table. "You don't look like Ezra Pound anymore," she said, sitting down opposite him.

He shook his napkin out and spread it on his lap. "At my age, I may be better off looking like myself," he said. It occurred to him that shaving the beard had turned out a perfect, if unplanned, diversion: Doris hadn't said a word about the dentist.

And until she did, neither would he.

21

STILL GRUMBLING ABOUT the loss of his beard although she'd had seventeen hours to get used to it, Doris had gone for a walk, and Davis-Williams sat on the back porch with his yellow pad on his knee, contemplating Rozlynne Haddad's questions.

What about that burglary? He'd entirely forgotten it, himself: when he went upstairs, as he'd better do soon, he'd have to enter it on the Monday morning page of his time sheets. Could Anita have seen something suspicious? Something she had talked about, without being aware of its significance? Her journal made no mention of any such thing, although it gave an amusing account of The Body and the stars. What about her "boyfriend," to use Roz's egregious term? Could she have written something in a letter to him that she hadn't put into her journal? He scribbled a note to himself to ask, next time he had occasion to talk to Ellis.

And Martin? He winced as his mind shied away from his mental image of the man, and he sighed and stretched his legs. This evening he could announce that he was walking over to the Tom Thumb on some pretext, stop at the house on Vincent to talk to Ellis. Yes. A self-inflicted pain, that would be, like pouring hot coffee into an ulcerated stomach, and possibly one that made less sense. For, surely, the police had thought of this? Would have asked? Would have taken any such letter away with them?

At the front of the house, the cover of the mail slot

clanked. He got up and went through the hall to collect the letters from the floor of the closet into which the slot opened. Too many bills, a new *New Yorker,* and another fat piece of somebody's journal. Two fat pieces, really; the return address showed both Sue's and Miriam's names. He carried the envelope and the magazine up to his kingdom and shut the door. Good Lord, he discovered, tearing open the envelope, they'd sent him the originals! The magazine he had clamped under his elbow fell to the floor and he scooped it onto the stack of others he meant to get around to reading, one of these days, and sat down at his desk.

Reading the cover letter, he had the nagging sense that he ought to know which of them had written it, but the two had become almost interchangeable in his mind and the letter was signed by both. Surely that reflected poorly upon his vaunted sensitivity (again!), to confuse the two women simply because they always seemed to be together?

To his vast surprise, the journals were not interchangeable. From Miriam, he got Weltschmertz. Deep Yearnings. The Meaninglessness of Life. The Desperation of Not Comprehending Infinity. Fixated at the age of twelve, he diagnosed, and why had she sent him all this? He remembered Dorothy LaBruyere's futile black marks. Miriam could have used the same good sense, he thought irritably. Had the girl no feeling for propriety?

Sue's, on the other hand, was just the gossipy sort of diary he had hoped for. He was cheered to find the source of Carlotta McCready's rage confirmed as The Body's entrancement of her husband—young fool—and astonished at being reminded that Jack Saarinen, The Wimp, had also succumbed to Roz's charms. That, Sue told her Dear Diary, was what Roz and Anita had argued about, after lunch on the day Anita was killed. And Sue, whose prurient interests seemed greatly overdeveloped, had more to say of others of the poets than she could possibly have known, surely? All sheer speculation, no doubt. Except . . .

Except that one of the beards had tried to sell her some cocaine. Had been sent away with a flea in his ear. "I," Sue said of herself, "at least have enough sense not to go to the cops about it, at least until I'm sure he's tried it on somebody else." What did that mean? If anything?

Swallowing his puzzlement, he read on. "T.C." he saw, in several places, twice circled and once garnished with exclamation points. What could *that* mean? Sue gave no explanation.

The woman was an instrument of mischief, that much was clear. Marybeth Saarinen would never have suspected Jack of wandering had not Sue been pleased to tell her, and crow in her diary about the "huff" in which the hapless woman had returned to St. Paul. Disgusting. . . .

And Sue, who didn't seem to like many people, including Miriam, had been positively gleeful at the result of tipping off Carlotta McCready to her husband's attentions to Roz—judged, apparently, on the basis of his having offered The Body a cigarette while they waited in Coleridge for the shuttle to Seven Slopes!

He skipped through the pages, forward and back, finding it all much of a muchness, until he tired of it. So much for lists of wildflowers, but it was what he had wanted, and at last he closed the drawer on Sue's diary, content enough that he stretched until his muscles quivered.

On the pretext of browsing among the magazines in the drugstore, he stopped that evening at the lavender house on Vincent Avenue. Cary Ellis had nothing to add. Anita had written—three letters—but nothing of the burglary or any other clandestine goings-on; if she'd seen anyone who shouldn't have been at Seven Slopes, she hadn't thought it worth mentioning.

Ellis sat on the couch, stroking the black and white cat with one hand and clutching a can of beer in the other. Davis-Williams had finished his own beer and sat nervously crushing the can. His excuse of a trip to the store for a magazine was wearing thinner every minute. "I have to go," he repeated.

Ellis gave him an almost timid glance. "What about Anita's poems? How are you coming on that?"

Her poems! How could he have forgotten? "Coming along," he temporized. "There aren't many, as you said. It will have to be a chapbook."

Ellis nodded. "Like a pamphlet, you mean."

"Er, yes, but a little fancier. I'll need permission from her heirs to publish, too—I'd forgotten that."

"That's her sister. No problem. I'll get her to write you a letter." Ellis tilted his can for the last few drops. "Oh, I was wondering. Do you think it should be under her maiden name?" The man's strained voice belied the casual words.

Her *maiden name!* Davis-Williams retrieved his chin. "Er, perhaps. I hadn't realized she was married."

"Oh, she wasn't. I mean, the guy's dead. A long time ago. They were only married a couple of months when he went overseas . . . he was a helicopter pilot, went down in Vietnam . . . so I wondered . . . it's Nelson."

"Her maiden name?" Ellis nodded. "Nelson," Davis-Williams repeated. "Excellent." He'd call Bill Weatherby at Fine Lines in the morning, twist his arm a little. *Anita Nelson?* He'd write a blurb for the inside front cover. *Nelson!* "Could I have a photo for the cover?" he asked.

"You could have that one." Ellis nodded toward the bookshelf.

Anita's gray eyes, her small smile surviving the commerciality of the photo, looked back at him. "I'd need permission from the photographer," he demurred.

"Oh, that's me," Ellis said. Sprawled lazily against the pillows of the couch . . . divan . . . bed . . . with the cat on his knee, he stared at the photo and blinked rapidly several times.

"It looks professional."

"It should. That's my job."

"Well." Davis-Williams began to wonder whether he could have become drunk on just one beer. "Thanks for the beer," he said.

"Sure." Ellis didn't move.

He found his own way out and down the stairs. Cudgel his brain as he might, he'd thought of no plausible excuse for an hour's absence and beer on his breath by the time he got home, so he decided to take a leaf from the day before and say nothing.

Doris met him at the door. "Well?" she demanded. "Where have you been?"

"I—ah—met one of my old students and had a beer with him."

"Oh? In the lot at the Tom Thumb, sitting on the back wall with the rest of the burnouts?"

"No," he said. "Of course not."

"You missed getting your magazine," she pointed out.

"They didn't have anything I wanted." He sidled around her and started up the stairs.

"Where are you going?"

"Up to my study. I've work to do."

"Can't it wait?"

He turned on the stairs and looked over the banisters at her upraised face. "No."

"You're quite sure it wasn't the dentist you met!" she shouted as he closed the door to his kingdom and leaned against it.

Really, he ought to tell her what he was doing. But she

would spoil it somehow, of that he was sure. Maybe he could tell her about the chapbook, as a sort of hush puppy. So easy to make a fool of himself at this novel, he thought, putting his face in his hands. So easy to fail. Another failure in the face of his wife. . . . No. No. No. He rubbed his face hard. She'd want to see the manuscript for the Guggenheim book, see for herself that it was all but done. And then she'd think of something else to do with "all that lovely time," drive to the Black Hills and visit those gawdawful people, or two weeks in Nassau when the weather turned dreary.

Six days later, a disquieting telephone call from Bill Weatherby:

"Who's this Nelson girl, Owen? A relative of some kind?"

What an extraordinary question! "No, no relation," he said. "Why do you ask?"

A sound that could only be described as a titter came over the line. "She good in bed?"

"Good God, what a question!" he protested, aloud this time. "I never slept with her, if that's what you're thinking."

"Oh. Beg pardon." The clatter of a typewriter filled a brief pause, and continued as Weatherby said, "You wouldn't want to rewrite this intro a little, then, would you?"

Davis-Williams didn't reply.

"I mean, it's a little extreme . . . I mean, the stuff isn't awful, I see lots worse in print every day, hell, I've printed some myself—and it's a couple of cuts above what comes over the transom. . . ."

"We'll keep the introduction as it is," Davis-Williams said stiffly.

"Well, it's your nickel, so I guess you can say what you like, but think it over, hey?"

"It's staying," he said recklessly.

"Suit yourself. The copy won't go to the typesetter for a couple of days, so if you change your mind, give me a ring, hey?"

"I won't change my mind. She's dead."

"Oh, that one." He heard Weatherby sucking at his teeth. "Maybe you could say something about it, then."

"Maybe."

But he didn't, and the weather turned cold as he worked every day at the novel, fumbling for phrases, writing, rewriting, sometimes ten or twelve times before he could go on, backtracking, revising. He erased the whole reel of tape he'd been using and started over again. The lindens at his elbow turned yellow, then bare; he could see into the street again, where the first evanescent snow of the season blew along the gutters with the brown leaves, and the younger children no longer rode their bicycles.

Bill Weatherby sent page proofs of Anita's chapbook and he corrected them carefully, admiring Bill's choice of typeface, his elegant layout of the book. He showed the proofs to Doris, who was as unimpressed as she had been when first told of the project, and as anxious that his own work not be neglected.

But: the novel. Each day's number of pages written was smaller than the last, as his puzzlement about how to deal with the unbelievable problem of Martin grew. He began to open the desk drawer each morning with a vague terror that this would be the day when nothing, nothing at all, came to mind to write down.

He sent another letter to the students who had sent their journals, thanking them and returning the various pages. He wrote again to the ones who hadn't responded, men, mostly, and asked again if they'd share their memories. Perhaps they hadn't kept journals. Perhaps they, the men, thought the keeping of journals unmasculine, or perhaps thought he had some untoward purpose.

The day came that he wrote nothing.

At Doris's behest, he let his beard grow in.

One morning, he saw in the newspaper a familiar face: a tiny, pinched mouth between pads of fat. He stared at it, punching at his mind, without luck. Then he read the story: a series of resort burglaries. The face came back, nibbling daintily at toast in the dining room at Seven Slopes that first day, the morning after the burglary. Yes. Seven Slopes was on the list of resorts burglarized by this man.

He called Sheriff Winton, to congratulate him on solving that case and to ask about "the Soderstrom affair," and found the man as stuck as he was himself. Not even apologetic about it. Not even holding out hope.

Still, he had hope. He could write again, starting at the place he'd begun to slow, and then, with just a little luck, he'd have one of those experiences he'd overheard other writers talking about, where the characters became so real that they took over and wrote the book by themselves. And then he would know. He would finally *know*.

In the space of three minutes, everything changed.

He had taken one of his usual Thursday evening walks to the library, carrying his books in a crocheted string bag his sister had sent him from Papua-New Guinea.

"I hear you're working on a new book," the woman at the checkout desk said. "When's it coming out?"

He jumped. How did she know? Oh, the sonnets. "I expect to get the finished manuscript to my publisher in April," he said. "And then it will be a few more months. It should be out in time for Christmas of next year."

"That long!" she marveled. "Not like those paperbacks on the Falkland Islands war that came out the day the shooting stopped.''

"No, poetry's more leisurely," he agreed. He smiled in his new beard and slipped the books she'd charged out into the bilum bag. They chatted a minute longer, he much enjoying the intelligent attention of this pleasant woman, until someone came up beside him with a stack of romances to take out. He glanced at the volumes in mild despair and went down the inside steps and through the door. Behind him, a man in a plaid wool jacket hastily thrust a book back into a shelf and clattered down the steps after him.

Davis-Williams didn't notice. Moving aside on the concrete outer steps to let a man and a small child pass, he turned right onto the dark sidewalk and strode peacefully toward the street lamp on the corner of Washburn Avenue, where he turned right in the blue light and strolled north on the dark side of the street. Still behind him, the man in the plaid jacket held the door open for the child, descended the library steps, and faded into a shadow that slipped from one thickening of darkness to the next.

Davis-Williams began to whistle something by Mozart and picked up his pace a bit as the jaunty rhythm infected his steps. The librarian's interest in his book returned as a small visual vignette of the light falling across her sharp features. How unimportant his sonnets seemed to him now! He imagined reading them as a stranger: why should he care how Owen Davis-Williams felt on stepping into a lake or watching the tilt of herring gulls against the wind? How much better to step into the cold shock of the lake oneself, to hear the gulls' *scree-scree* with one's own ears!

His whistling and his thoughts served to cover any sound but his own. In the middle of the dim block, the shadow made its rush.

He heard the hurried footsteps close behind him an instant too late. Half turned, lips still relaxing from his whistle, he caught the weight of the rush on his right side. The books in the bag over his shoulder slammed into his ribs, forcing a harsh gasp of pain from his throat. He staggered into the gutter between two parked cars with a half-formed *what?*

The shadow launched again. Davis-Williams went down, grunting among the acrid leaves. The momentum rolled him over; the books dug into his back. He tried to call for help, but only a strangled *oh!* came out. A hand pressed across his mouth and nose before he could take another breath, cutting off the air. His whole attention shifted to drawing breath against that pressure. Another hand fumbled at the neck of his jacket. Cold fingers touched his throat. His belly melted in fear.

A car revved up Washburn. In its reflected lights he saw a face, absolutely that of a stranger: long-nosed, weak-chinned, a wide mouth gasping above a gray and black blankety-looking jacket. He tried again to wrench himself to his feet, but only the string bag went flying, out past the line of the parked cars into the street. Library books. Have to replace them.

The car screeched to a stop. The man rose and fled. Davis-Williams scrambled to his feet. "Stop!" he shouted. "Stop!" The second *stop* came out a winded gargle: he stumbled against a fender and pushed himself erect, the faint sparks of dizziness glowing against the ground.

Two teenaged boys flew out of the back doors of the car that had stopped and pounded after the running man. He heard one yell, "This way," from someone's backyard. And then there were a few more shouts, a silence, a wait in which he gathered the spilled books, dirty but undamaged. A porch light went on across the street, but no one came out to investigate. The boys came back.

"He got away," the taller one said. "Hey, that was neat. Friend of yours?"

"No."

"What'd he get?"

"Nothing."

"I guess you lucked out, huh? Geez, you look rotten," the boy commented breezily. "Want a ride?"

"Yes, thanks," he managed, still breathing painfully. The inside of the car was sweet with pot smoke, the boys cheerful and grandiose. One might almost think they'd caught the lout.

They let him off in front of his house, giggling warnings about taking candy from strangers, and peeled rubber making the turn into the next block. Feeling more battered than he was, he stumbled up the front steps and felt for the lock with his key.

"What on earth?" Doris jumped up as he entered the sitting room. "What's happened? You've got a leaf in your hair!"

"Somebody tried to mug me," Davis-Williams replied, putting his hand to the door frame to steady himself. He shuddered off the memory of the cold hand at his throat.

"What's that smell? It smells like marijuana!"

"It is marijuana," he said. "Some kids gave me a ride home. The car was full of it."

"Honestly, Owen, have you no sense at all?" Doris asked. "Suppose the police had stopped them? Or suppose they had crashed the car?"

"Two blocks," he said fiercely.

"Sometimes I wonder if you're fit to be let out," she persisted.

"Oh, leave me alone!" He stamped up the stairs and slammed the door to his study, an effect rather dampened by the weather-stripping, and stood in the center of the room catching his breath.

After a moment he brushed the leaf out of his hair and

212

let the string bag slide off his shoulder. Wearily, he unzipped his jacket. A scrunch of paper bounced to the floor.

Heart still hammering, he picked it up and teased it open with his fingernails pinching only the very edges of the paper. In letters cut from a newspaper and neatly pasted along a faintly ruled line, he read:

FOR YOUR OWN GOOD, STOP WRITING FICTION!!!!

It was, of course, unsigned.

22

THE SENSIBLE THING would have been to go back downstairs and call the Minneapolis police. Instead, Davis-Williams took off his jacket and pulled up his sweater and undershirt to examine the damage. One small bruise over his ribs, book-corner-shaped, and what felt like another bruise coming on his right shin. Not much.

When he thought again about the fingers at his throat, he realized that they had been stuffing the paper down the front of his jacket, not trying to choke him. So it seemed no actual harm had been intended. But why choose so dramatic a method of delivery? Why not simply entrust the note to the post office?

He walked slowly to his desk and sat down, holding the paper by one corner. Ah. A second message had also been delivered: I know how you live. I can find you when I choose to.

At the thought he got up to pull the shades, something he almost never did. He wanted to look out into the dark street, to see if someone perhaps loitered on the sidewalk, but found himself afraid to. A little sifting of dust came down as he tugged on the shade-pull.

He sat down at his desk and rolled paper into his typewriter: a letter to Sheriff Winton describing the incident. He rummaged through his desk drawers to find a large manila envelope, and put the letter and the note, clipped backside-to to the letter, into the envelope. He didn't think he'd touched the back of the message in smoothing it. He wished he could remember.

214

"Open with care," he printed across the face and the back of the envelope, stamped his return address on the upper left-hand corner, looked out the sheriff's address and wrote that on. Postage should be somewhere in the top left-hand drawer. Another round of rummaging brought forth a book of eighteen-cent stamps showing big-horned sheep; he put two of them on the envelope with the obscure feeling that their small size somehow cheated him, and sat back with a deeply drawn breath.

Now for Doris.

He slipped the letter into the center drawer of his desk and went downstairs to face the dragon.

She was sitting upright in one of the chintz-covered chairs that faced the fireplace in the living room; the embers of a fire glowed and she had a book on her lap, but her cheeks were streaked with tears and she wouldn't look at him.

"Dee?"

She shook her head violently. "Owen, what's going on?" she asked, in a voice high with despair.

"Very little." Sinking into the other chair, he leaned his forearms on his knees, hands clasped. "Nothing you need worry about."

"I'm not so much worried as hurt."

He thought that over with mild befuddlement and found nothing to say.

"I thought that with the fellowship, and I know you've got at least half of your book done already—had it done, before the summer—I arranged to teach just the one class—I thought—" She glanced quickly up at him and away. "I thought there'd be time to do some of the things we've left off doing—but you're up there in that room *all the time*—it can't all be that wretched girl's poetry—sixteen poems you haven't even to change a word of? Don't you have any time for me?"

"Oh, Dee." He sighed. "What kind of things did you have in mind to do?" he asked, in resignation.

"Remember? One time you started to teach me Welsh, and then our teaching loads got too heavy to do that and poetry too, and we stopped. I'd thought we might take that up again?"

"Doris, that was years ago!" Yet the pink glow of the dying fire on her cheek was the same: odd, when the cheek itself had grown lined.

"Yes, but couldn't we still? And we haven't been to the Art Institute or the Walker once since we came back to town, there's the Science Museum in St. Paul I wanted to see, they remodeled the Como Park Zoo ages ago and we've never been, the zoo in Apple Valley has new exhibits—"

"That's what you want to do? Go to a zoo?"

She turned her tear-streaked face toward him and nodded slightly. "And other things, Owen. The Guthrie's new season looks fascinating, or we could go to the flicks or a concert, have friends to dinner. . . ."

"My book needs a lot of work," he said dimly.

"Every day? Every evening?"

Ten minutes later he had committed himself to a day in St. Paul, thrice-weekly Welsh lessons, and a dinner party a week from the coming Saturday in preparation for which he had promised to help clean the house. He left Doris planning flowers for the centerpiece and went upstairs to retrieve a book from the bilum bag.

The next day he walked over to the little shopping area on Upton, this time with Doris's blessing. He posted the letter to Winton in the box by the drugstore and crossed kitty-corner to the butcher to pick up some chops for dinner, then recrossed the street to the Co-op to weigh out his own dried beans and brown rice and fill the clean jar Doris had sent with him with freshly ground peanut butter. The day was fine, warm enough to go about with his light jacket unzipped, and he walked home slowly, savoring the crisp fall air.

The mail had come while he was out, bringing with it a letter from Jack Saarinen saying sorry, he had no journal and would just as soon have no memories. Bad luck, that. Davis-Williams supposed Rozlynne Haddad was responsible. He thought of the girl, alternating between braces and swimming pool, and wondered what she did for exercise, now that the pool was surely drained for the winter, with oak leaves drifting into its corners. Already, the geese were gathering at Lake Calhoun. In three weeks they'd be gone, Thanksgiving only a fowl-fed recollection, December facing him with its icy stare. Difficult to believe.

Also in the mail was a little pink slip to tell him he could pick up a parcel at the post office the next day. That would be Anita's chapbooks. What rotten timing! Perhaps he could press Doris into helping him to address envelopes for sending off the review copies. If she felt useful, she might not feel so affronted, he reasoned; he shoved the pink slip into his pocket and carried the letter from Saarinen up to his kingdom.

Only one page of his "novel" that morning, and that only because of the attack of the night before. He thought with nostalgia and envy of the lickety-split pace of his first few weeks. Now, even rewriting had hit a snag: he had no idea what to say next. He'd wait for a reply from Sheriff Winton, he decided. Surely that message, delivered in that manner, must be a break!

The knife hadn't been a break, he recalled. All the deputies' questions hadn't helped. Davis-Williams stared out at the fat-budded linden twigs near his window. Lime trees, he thought. Lime trees. How had they got that name in England, having nothing to do with limes?

In his scattered fashion, he was still reading Dr. Skeat's etymological dictionary an hour later.

A full week passed, in which neither he nor the sheriff wrote a word, so far as Davis-Williams could tell. He had collected the package: Anita's chapbooks, just as he'd thought. Asking Doris to help had been a master stroke: she was all business, efficient beyond his wildest dreams; the review copies, all two hundred of them, were ready to mail in one day.

Late Friday afternoon, the sheriff called.

Doris came up to the study to fetch him to the telephone. "Owen, please be honest with me," she demanded, whispery and anxious. "You aren't in any difficulty with this man, are you?"

"No."

"Please, you'll tell me?"

"Of course, I'd tell you," he snapped. "Let me go talk to him. And don't hover."

She went downstairs and into the kitchen, where she banged the pans about while he took the telephone to the limit of its cord, round the wall into the living room.

"You gave me a busy week, Williams," the sheriff said.

"Oh?"

"That note was covered with fingerprints. Yours, mostly."

"Mine? How did you know they were mine?"

"We compared them with your cover letter, of course," Winton explained, as if to a child. "The others belonged to Edward James Moosman."

"Moose!"

Davis-Williams felt his knees begin to give. The scene outside the dining room at Seven Slopes flashed into his mind. If only he had told! Yet surely his assailant had been a stranger?

No. Not really. Now he understood why Doris had

been so very startled when he had shaved his own beard. The telephone cord hadn't stretched to a chair, so he sat tailor-fashion on the floor. "Oh, dear," he said. "I never suspected."

"No reason why you should."

Davis-Williams pictured the chap leaning back in his unsquealing swivel chair, the loops of the telephone cord bouncing as he moved. "Where did you get his fingerprints?" he asked, with visions of the sheriff sitting in that chair, directing his minions to follow the former students about with open inky pads and bits of paper.

"He was in the army, few years back. Not hard to match, since we didn't have many people to try for."

"You've arrested him, then?" That long, thin nose poked out between bars, the wide, thin-lipped mouth open in a soundless howl, the knobby fingers clamped around shafts of blue steel.

"No reason to," the sheriff said, "unless you've made a complaint."

"Complaint?"

"To the Minneapolis police," said Winton, very, very patiently. "You do have cops down there, don't you? People can call them, can't they? So, did you?"

"Did I?" Davis-Williams repeated, stupefied.

"After he rolled you, as you put it," in exasperation. "By the way, that usually means something like robbing a drunk."

"Oh. No, I didn't."

"Well, then there's no reason to arrest him."

"Wait a minute!" Davis-Williams found himself clutching the receiver with both hands. "Didn't he kill Anita?"

"Oh, no. We knew that."

"No! Then what was that all about?"

Winton sighed, a raspy blast in Davis-Williams's ear. "Keep this under your hat, will you? Mr. Moosman has some psychological difficulties. The method used to kill Mrs. Soderstrom"—even Winton knew she'd been married, Davis-Williams thought with a pang—"was one he learned and used in combat. So he was afraid he might have done it without knowing it. He once threw a tear gas canister into a noisy party, thinking it was a grenade he was throwing into a crowd of gooks, he says. He has nightmares where the things he saw and did in Vietnam are transferred to his friends and family."

The moment of revulsion at the epithet disappeared. "How horrid!" Davis-Williams exclaimed.

"Quite," Winton replied, mockingly. "Gave my investigator a lot of trouble. But we knew he couldn't have done it, even though some joker called him in the middle of the night up at Seven Slopes and said something that made him think he had."

"How did you know he, er, was innocent?"

"Other people accounted for him from the last time Mrs. Soderstrom was seen alive until after she was found. He was relieved to hear it."

"I should imagine." Alonzo the cat came up and sniffed at the apparition of Davis-Williams on the floor. He stretched out a finger and scratched absently under the beast's collar. "But, if it wasn't Moose, who was it?"

"Your guess is as good as mine. Maybe better. That's why I'm calling you—if Moose could figure that out, anybody could. You must have some key, something you don't know about or haven't figured out. So C.Y.A., as they used to say."

"I'm afraid I don't—"

"Cover your ass," the sheriff said genially, and hung up. I should be getting used to these abrupt good-byes by now, Davis-Williams thought, and scrambled to his feet. Not Moose. He stepped toward the hall and leaned against the door frame. Not Moose. Then Martin?

Kind, pedantic, pipe-smoking, gray-haired Martin? The thought made him sick.

Doris emerged from the kitchen as he cradled the phone. "Dinner's almost ready," she said. "Owen, what was that about?"

It wasn't fair to worry her so. He could see that. He could almost see his peace, his Guggenheim, flutter away like an old sheet of newspaper on the wind—but he would have to tell her, he'd have no peace or Guggenheim time if he didn't, either. So, while they set the table and sat down to dinner, he explained his project.

"That's why you've spent so much time upstairs? A novel about that girl's murder?"

She was so incredulous, he was almost insulted. He nodded.

"Oh, how could you!" she cried. "How could you spend all your time up there with her and leave me down here all alone? I'm your wife!"

The words took a moment to sink in, while he stared at her hands, tensed into fists, and her forehead, so tight it seemed as if a rake had been drawn across it. "Really, Doris," he protested. "Don't you think it a bit bizarre to be so jealous of a dead woman? You've forgotten the bread."

"Bizarre! Bizarre, is it?" She put her hands against the edge of the table, reared back and gave him her "British look," eyebrows up, nostrils flared to make little dents on either side of her nose. "Oh, yes, quite curious, most bizarre!" She laughed, her brittle horsey laugh, and got up from the table.

"Doris?"

She left the room, still laughing, while he sat on at his place and struggled to find her reference. Ah, yes. Ionesco. She was making fun of him with the allusion, he knew, but he couldn't quite see how. Nothing of those inane people applied to him, did it? He shook his head

221

and helped himself to buttered Brussels sprouts. He would never understand the woman, never, not if he lived with her to the age of ninety. Forty more years!

Doris returned, sobered, and plunked a plate of rolls down on the table. She sat down, took a roll, broke it open. He had the uncomfortable feeling that he should be saying something. What, he didn't know. They ate silently for several minutes. "But you've not been writing the past few days," Doris said abruptly. "Are you finished, then?"

"No. Stuck."

"What do you mean, stuck?"

He gestured with his fork. "I thought that if I put together all the information I could gather, and wrote it up in a mystery-novel way, as I've been saying—a detective roman à clef, in the style of your P. D. James or the Marsh woman—"

Doris's eyebrows shot up, but she said nothing.

"Something of the kind, anyway," he said, stung without knowing why. "Have you ever heard of character possession?"

Her eyes slewed toward him, and she swallowed. "No."

He leaned across his plate, eager to explain. "It's when you've thought out your characters so well, they become almost like real people. They do things you haven't thought up for them to do, they behave—they make up the book for you, in a way—take over and write it, I've heard. So I thought, if I wrote well and truly, the characters in this book would take over and show me, well, which of them did it."

Doris maintained the same odd stare. "But, Owen," she objected. "These are real people."

"Yes, but—"

"You can't know them as well as characters that spring from your own mind. Just can't."

"But if I knew them well enough—"

She stood and picked up her plate. "You can't."

He watched her bump open the kitchen door with her hip. What did she know? She was a botanist, not a writer. He trapped his silverware under his thumb against the plate and carried them into the kitchen.

"You could be right," he conceded. "Because I am stuck. That leaves only two things I can do, I guess."

She wrenched the hot water tap on and squeezed a stream of dishwashing soap into the sink. "What?"

"I could start all over again from the very beginning. I don't have all the journals anymore, but I do have Anita's and mine. I have the information from all those others written down on my time sheets. I can go through, chapter by chapter, and see if I left anything important out. Perhaps you'd like to help with that?"

Doris glanced sideways and shuddered. "How ghoulish! No."

"And then—this I would have to do by myself, I'm afraid—just begin writing again, more slowly this time, and see if the original plan will work."

"Or?"

"Or I can send the manuscript and the yellow pad to the sheriff and see if they suggest anything to him. In fact, I can do both! I'll take everything over to the print shop tomorrow and have them run off copies."

"At fifteen cents a page?"

He responded with a cavalier flourish of his right hand. "It's only a couple of hundred pages of typescript so far, and about thirty of the time sheets."

Doris shook her head again and sighed deeply. "Who's your main candidate for the honor of villain?"

Martin, he was about to say, but couldn't bring himself to do it. "None, alas."

At that, she smiled, the smile of a mother whose toddler has done something illicitly cute, and said,

"There's a cheesecake in the fridge. Would you cut us some? And pour the kettle over the coffee, it's all set up."

He poured boiling water into the top of the drip pot and took the cheesecake out of the refrigerator. "Oh, lovely," he said, salivating.

Doris put cups on a tray, and the slices of cheesecake with red cherry topping dribbling slowly down their sides beside them, and carried everything into the living room. "Poke up the fire, would you, Owen?" she asked, setting the tray on the table in front of the couch. "And get me a glass of brandy. I feel I need it, somehow."

They had one glass of brandy each, and talked, he wasn't sure why, of their early days in Cambridge. An argument over the habits of swans was settled with recourse to their old *Britannica*. Whether it was the warm glow of the brandy, the discussion, or the trip into a happier past, he didn't know, but when Doris had turned out the bedside lamp he passed his hand over her belly with the first stirring of real desire he'd had for her in many days. She was startled when his lips found hers; he felt her draw back in surprise and then respond, and he pressed harder against her, kissed her closed eyes, burrowed his nose into the warm groove of her neck.

Afterward, he lay with Doris in his arms, contented as he had been as a younger man, and sleepily listened to the calls of geese high over the moonlit house until he drowsed off.

He dreamed that Moose had got into the house somehow. With a steak knife filched from the dining room at Seven Slopes, the former commando flowed from shadow to shadow in the moonstruck house, until the knife caught the cold light and blazed. Fire! Fire! But no, it was all right; he needn't get up: the chap swept the fire neatly into the fireplace and nothing was damaged; he fled, dropping his flat sandals, which Davis-Williams stuffed into the bilum bag and tidied into the hall closet. All was well. All was well.

He woke to the smell of frying bacon and went downstairs in his dressing gown to greet his wife with a peck on her cheek. She smiled at him, wanly, he thought, and turned to the stove for the skillet.

"What beautiful eggs!" he exclaimed, genuinely impressed. Doris seldom troubled to cook eggs this way, gently, basted with the hot bacon grease to cloud the white over the yolk. It was the egg photographed for the menu at Seven Slopes but never once served to him there, the egg his Mam had cooked in an iron pan over a coal stove in the chilly mornings of his childhood, the egg he had never contrived to produce for himself in thirty years of trying.

Doris smiled again, the same half smile. She put three rashers of bacon on the plate beside the eggs and reached over his shoulder (her hands still smelling of the rubber gloves she'd worn to wash the pan) to set the plate before him.

"You must have been up for ages," he said.

"Long enough." She glanced over her shoulder at him on her way to the sink. So much he could never know of her. The precise pressure of her hand against the faucet, her slow, silent count to twenty to measure the water into the kettle, just sufficient to pour into the pot and fill it nicely.

Owen grinned happily. This was like a return to youth, Doris up early and puttering about, himself a lie-about sprawled on the bed, then coming to the kitchen to be fed.

She sat opposite him with her tea. "I think I'll cut the mums back this morning," she said. "They're nearly done, and we'll soon have real snow, not that teasing stuff we had in October."

"Right." He peppered his eggs.

"Then the shopping," she said. "And dinner tonight's all set to go. Do you think we'd have time to go out to a park and tramp about a bit?"

He looked up, struck by the flatness of her tone. "If that's what you'd like to do."

She nodded, not looking at him.

By the time he had eaten his breakfast and gone up to dress, Doris was out hacking away at the fading chrysanthemums. He was leisurely about dressing, pleased with his jeans, faded to the precise shade of blue he favored, and his Mexican shirt. He'd take the manuscript over to copy while she was shopping, he decided, and send the whole thing to Winton to make of what he could. First, perhaps, read over the first chapter or two to see whether the tape recorder would tell him, this time, something his eye could not. Get a start on rewriting, before Doris's tramp. Yes.

Yawning still, he crossed the upstairs hall to his kingdom, threaded the tape recorder, and snapped it on with one hand as he opened the center drawer of his desk with the other.

And stared.

The manuscript was gone.

23

HE GAPED AT the empty space for a full minute before he understood what he saw. "What can I have done with the thing?" he asked himself aloud.

He banged through the other drawers of the desk in search of the stack of cheap typing paper. Everything else was as he'd left it: the poetry manuscript in its black binder, the notes for the introduction he'd written to Anita's chapbook, the yellow pad—the yellow pad wasn't as he'd left it. The sheets with the time notes had been torn away.

"What on earth?" he asked himself. He straightened up and looked round the room, at the shelves and the file cabinet, the stacked glossy magazines—ah! He'd been reading both together, magazines and manuscript, just yesterday. He tore through the stack, scattering the magazines over the floor, but the manuscript wasn't among them. Where, then?

He let his eyes go round the room again, and then the meaning of the contents of the fireplace leaped at him. Not the white ash of a fire let die, that. Little black leaves, stirred with the poker. Burnt paper.

He dashed for the door, cursed as he slipped on one of the magazines, ripped open the door with such force that it shuddered loudly in his hand. "Doris!" he bellowed. "Doris, where are you?"

Out with the mums, he remembered, and started down the stairs. But there she was at the bottom, looking up at him with her mouth slack as an imbecile's. Somehow that slack mouth added to his outrage: the wave of anger that came up from his bowels frightened him.

"Doris, come here," he said, stiffening his belly against his rage.

She ducked her head and scurried up the stairs, and followed him into his study.

"What have you done to my new book?" he asked, very distinctly.

She raised her chin and looked down her nose. "I took it out of your desk and burned it." He could hear the ashes stirring in the fireplace as she spoke, crisp little whispers in the draft from open door through open damper. He couldn't think why he hadn't heard the sound before.

"Why?"

"I'm tired of it."

"Two months' work!" he squealed.

Her cheeks, never beautiful, had two blotchy red patches on them that deepened as he watched, half detached, half in horror. "Two months' work you never should have done," she retorted. "All day, all evening, day after day after day, I had to sit down there by myself, and you up here with your door closed, so well sealed I have to shout to be heard when I'm standing just outside. It's humiliating!"

Her anger stunned him. He couldn't reply.

"All this time, all these years, *I've* worked, *I've* shopped and cooked and cleaned, *I've* tidied your messes, so you wouldn't have to think of it all, all this mundane stuff you've no patience for—"

"My work, Doris," he said, baffled. Wait, he remembered. There's a second copy in the file cabinet—

"Not your work," Doris snapped. "Your work is poetry. Poetry! Not this senseless chronicle of the unremarkable death of an unremarkable woman—" Her voice trembled and she stopped.

228

"She was murdered!" he shouted.

"Yes!" Doris shrieked. "Murdered! And a lot of good it did me!"

"Did you?" he asked, into the silence that followed her outburst.

She misunderstood. "Yes," she said. "I did."

He gaped at her, speechless.

"You oaf, you were so besotted with her, they were talking about it at breakfast. Laughing!" Tears crawled down the vertical creases of her cheeks. "How do you think I felt, watching them snigger when I came in? One of them even called me on the telephone while you were gone, one lunchtime, to tell me you were with *her!*"

T. C., he thought suddenly. *Telephone call.* Suzanne Falk. Bitch.

"What do you think that did to me?" Doris pounded her chest with the bunched fingers of both hands, so that he stepped forward to grasp her wrists, to prevent her hurting her breasts.

"Doris, calm down, do," he said, in his most sensible voice. "How could you have killed her? You were having one of your headaches."

"I thought it would end there," she sobbed. "I meant never to tell you. But no, you had to go on and on—ever since, you've thought of nothing but her, her work, her precious little life—"

"Doris, you're deluding yourself," he insisted. "You can't have killed her. I saw you in bed just before I went to class, myself, and afterward, when I came back, you were still there, asleep. You dreamed it."

Doris tittered. "You idiot! I swiped a wig from Judy Ammans and made up a bundle of bedclothes, just in case you looked in. Just as they do for prison escapes!"

"Wig?"

"And then I nipped out the side door and down the back paths. She was sitting on *our bench,*" Doris continued, sounding shocked. Her eyes looked past him, past the wall. "I sat beside her. I said, 'Isn't that a black-and-white warbler?' and the fool girl looked where I pointed. I had the knife ready in my bag. I pulled it out and stabbed her—I've read how, often enough! It worked! It worked! She didn't even cry out!" Doris laughed, the laughter of unexpected triumph.

"Doris—"

"And then up the hill and down through the studio—pity about the jar, I didn't know it would ruin it—and into the room. I wasn't gone ten minutes. The next morning I shoved the wig under the bed in Ammans's room, where Judy would think it had been kicked, or one of those beastly little brats had hidden it."

Dear Lord, she was serious! She believed this claptrap! "Doris, how could a woman like you even think herself capable of such a thing?"

"Oh, Owen," she said, shaking her head. "Only you would think I couldn't. Only a man who cooks up a mad scheme like that book you've been writing could miss so much about a woman he's lived with so long."

In coming all the way into the room he had made a grave mistake, he now saw. He would have to pass Doris to get out of the room, to the telephone.

"And Rozlynne Haddad?" he asked, with sudden suspicion.

"That didn't work so well, did it?" she said ruefully. "I gave her a shove. I thought I could twist her neck when I got down the stairs, but you were in the way and I wasn't quick enough."

"Doris, why?" he cried.

Again she misunderstood. "I'd already got rid of one woman to keep you," she said reasonably. "D'you think I'd stand by and lose you to another?"

"Dear God!" he exclaimed. He edged around the magazines, making for the door.

"Where are you going?"

How could she ask? Stand there in her mud-colored skirt and shapeless wool jumper, still, he saw with shock, holding the gardening gloves in one hand, and ask such a question? "To call the doctor."

"The doctor!"

Ears burning, he remembered the many times he'd failed her, turned away her advances, over the summer. The heat. . . . "I don't know why you've developed this delusion," he said. "Perhaps last summer's heat. But you need some kind of help." Good Lord, how trite that sounded. "So I'm going to call Dr. Haynes, see what he has to say."

"No!" She dropped the gloves and put out her hands. "Owen, don't you see? I did it for us, so that we could be together again, like last night!"

"I'm telephoning," he said firmly.

"No!" Doris screeched. She snatched up the poker from the hearth. "He'll have them put me away! He'll call the police! They'll lock me up! What about our dinner party? What about our tramp in the park?"

"Doris, put the poker down," he said, as he might to a small child getting out of hand. "I'm going to call—"

She rushed at him, poker raised. He tried to sidestep, a shrill moan of fear escaping his locked throat, and she turned to intercept him. Skidded on a magazine. Crashed to the floor. Her head hit the corner of the raised brick hearth with a sickening thunk, and her eyes flew open. Her back twitched.

He didn't stop to investigate. He ran down the stairs, so fast he almost stumbled, called for police and ambulance, his fingers fumbling the seven digits into the dial. "Quickly, quickly," he implored the calm female voice that answered.

He yanked open the front door and left it standing wide, cold clean air rushing into the house, and ran back

231

up the stairs. Doris was still alive, her breath harsh and irregular. Dying. *To my wife, without whom.* He didn't try to touch her. His chest seemed frozen, and then his throat broke open with a harsh cry and he began to sob, holding on to the door frame.

Much later, after the careening ride in the ambulance, the tense wait, the policeman on the bench beside him asking so many questions, he returned to what had been his kingdom. From the doorway he heard a strange ticking sound, a sound he'd heard before but couldn't place. He took two timid steps into the room and listened carefully, and then he saw what it was: the free end of the recording tape flipping round and round the reel.

Relief. Shame at his relief. Everything Doris had said that morning was recorded on that tape: he was safe. No one could blame him for her death, or for any other.

He turned slowly, surveying his late kingdom, from the bare ruined choirs of the linden branches tapping at the windows, past the locked filing cabinet to the weather-stripping on the door. He wasn't safe, not really. He could see that now. Not from his own mind, already busy with guilt, going *if . . . if . . . if. . .* like the flapping end of the tape.